M: The Mystical Odyssey Of Harriet E. Wilson

Alison Clarke

For information address:
Oprelle Publications,
236 Twin Hills Rd.
Grindstone, PA 15442.

FIRST EDITION

ISBN: 979-8-9899015-9-3

*To Mom and Dad for their never-ending support,
the Aunts, Aunt Ada, Aunt Lottie, and Auntie
Louise who always knew,
and Conor who always believed.*

Praise for M — The Mystical Odyssey of Harriet E. Wilson

"When Harriet E. Wilson – a young Black writer born into a world that denies her story – finds herself caught up in a realm where magic and memory intertwine, she is forced to face the ghosts of her past in order to discover her truest power. In this reimagining of the life of America's first Black woman novelist, Alison Clarke weaves an intriguing tale of imagination and courage. Guided by ancestral spirits and her own strong will, Harriet discovers that her voice can defy time itself. If you love Octavia Butler, you will find The Mystical Odyssey of Harriet E. Wilson to be an illustrious, empowering journey through history and the heart – a celebration of survival, storytelling, and Black girl magic."

—Latorial Faison, Poet, Virginia State University Professor; Chair of The Department of Languages; Literature, Pulitzer Prize Nominee, Author of Nursery Rhymes in Black, Mother to Son, The Missed Education of the Negro: An Examination of the Black Segregated Education Experience in Southampton County, 1950-1970

"The Mystical Odyssey of Harriet E. Wilson takes the reader on a journey through time, spectrums and cultures to the fantastical locales where stories began, grew, and grow still, often interacting and developing into new tales and prophecies. What we discover is that all is not well in the lands of the legendary. Goddesses, heroes and magical beasts find themselves threatened by the evil forces of oppression seeking to silence them. Though often triumphant in their battle against the rising tide of darkness, the leading characters learn they need to make contact with The Messenger or face eradication. But before that can happen, The Messenger must discover her own identity, learn to navigate a difficult reality, and find the courage to pursue her path or be unable to reach and serve others. This is a story of stories, the voices they speak with, the truth they offer and the timeless realms they come from and create within us."

—Joan Crate, Poet and author of Black Apple

"Alison Clarke's novel about Harriet E. Wilson – the first person of colour to publish a novel in 1859 – melds historical fiction, prose, poetry, and fantastical elements to a further understanding about women of colour artists. Women like Harriet E. Wilson forged their own paths artistically, and became trailblazers."

—Adriana A. Davies
CM, Cav. d'Italia, PhD
Historian and Poet

"As promised by its title, Alison Clarke's novel takes readers on a "mystical odyssey "which not only acclaims Harriet Wilson but a whole empowered cast of Sisterhood characters as well. This narrative goes beyond world-building to galaxy-expanding travel in a magical journey that celebrates gendered solidarity and appreciates how role models from our past can help us imagine shared futures."

—Sarah Ruffing Robbins, co-director of "The Genius of Phillis Wheatley Peters"; author of Learning Legacies: Archive to Action through Women's Cross-Cultural Teaching; coeditor of The Lives, Writings, and Legacies of Phillis Wheatley Peters and Transatlantic Anglophone Literatures.

"Immersive. Takes you right into tales wide and deep, shimmering and dark. Transports you into Clarke's imagining of Harriet E. Wilson's imagination. You engage with beings real and mythical, of this and other worlds."

—Rona Altrows,
2025 Winner, The Prairie Grindstone Prize

"Alison Clarke is an accomplished poet and novelist and has brought to life an amazing fantasy world in celebration of Harriet E. Wilson. Her opening chapter, situated in Elk Island Park, a place very dear to me, brought it so close to home, and then her use of colour and descriptive prose inspired my imagination. This beautiful work of fiction will touch your heart and open your mind to endless possibilities."

—Carolyn Cordell
President, Parkland Poets

"Alison Clarke takes readers on a journey across times in the company of luminous wisewomen, Aziza faeries, sister sirens, twinned soothsayers, so many more – and the intrepid Harriet, Singer of Lyric Song. Drawing on Ashanti, Irish, and Greek folktales, Clarke's Odyssey illuminates the importance of a little-known 19th-century Black American writer."

—Joycelyn K. Moody
Sue E. Denman Distinguished
Chair in American Literature
Professor of English
University of Texas at San Antonio

"The Mystical Odyssey of Harriet E. Wilson is an enjoyable fast-paced journey that weaves mythologies across time and space. This epic tale explores themes of identity, resilience, and the magic of creativity. Richly imagined and deeply inspiring, this story is a celebration of art, memory, and the enduring power of story to unite and transform."

—Jody Sanders,
Vice-President, Parkland Poets

Chapter One:
Selena

LAND of golden silk. The earth. Granules of golden brown. Creatures flying in the air – sand creatures with fangs and eyes of glass – capped, with large goggles surrounding their ghastly glass eyes, and hoods that hid their faces. I saw these creatures in my dreams, night after night. I thought, "What did it mean?"

The next day, I decided to go to the park, Elk Island, home of the bison. More questions entered my mind, "They were so huge, these big beasts of dark brown fur and horns, but yet their bodies are on these little legs? How could such little legs hold up such big beasts?" It still boggled my mind. I asked myself, "How did Nature have such a purposeful design? How did that come into being? Is there something beyond us out there? What are the origins of the universe?"

Before you know it, I was out on one of the barbecue sites, not far from a lake, getting some wood from one of the nearby sheds and built a fire. I felt like roasting marshmallows, so I did. The fire, scarlet, framed with gold, and a base of cerulean, greeted me. I closed my eyes for a while, the fire cackled softly, but it was like a soft music. But then I sensed something: I knew that something was flying in the stratosphere, but close to me, and I didn't know what. Another question floated into my mind, "How did I know?" These things, it made me wonder – maybe there is something beyond us that we do not quite understand. Maybe. I kept closing my eyes and thinking of what could be. Then, I sensed something and opened them.

A huge spider appeared in front of me; I almost fainted. Suddenly, there was a ball of light: magenta, gold, emerald, and fuchsia. I again closed my eyes, afraid of what I might see. I opened them again, and in front of me was a woman, a tall woman with skin the colour of cocoa, and the most haunting but also sombre grey eyes. I didn't know what to say. Then, wings, butterfly wings, appeared out of nowhere. I didn't know what to believe.

"You," she said. I didn't say a word. "You," she repeated. "You," she echoed.

"What are you?" I gasped. "I've never seen anything like it. It's like I'm in a dream."

"Dream, it is not. I have only read about your kind – mortals. I know your feet touch the ground in many realms, in many lifetimes, past, present, and future, but here you are. I don't know what to think myself."

"Why are you here?"

"I don't know," replied the shape-shifter, "I got bored. There's nothing to do in my Kingdom where I'm from. It is not easy, this life of solitude; well, loneliness... I paid a high price for my pride."

I asked what she meant, and the faerie, who later said that her name was Anisie, told me. A king, King Jobali, punished her for having a beautiful gift: a gift of weaving beautiful clothes, like tunics shimmering with silver threads and embroidered with sapphires and rubies. Anisie also made dresses with the silk from her moon, Sutania, sister to our Moon. The silk made from Lady Sutania's rays illuminated the universe where Anisie lived.

Her shawls were made from Lady Sutania's moondrops that shimmered like pearls. But the King was jealous, and Anisie did not want to back down when he punished the artisans for creating Beauty that surpassed the artisans of his court. The other artisans, people Anisie knew, relented, following the King's demands and later a decree that only the artisans from the Royal Court could make such finery. But Anisie would not submit. She would not acquiesce. She would not back down, and so his sorcerer changed her into a spider, and now Anisie can only take human form in moonlight, or when she travels through space and time.

I replied quietly, "That's tough. What are you going to do now?"

"I have to stay steadfast in my solitude, traverse the universe, or rather universes, and learn. You? Are you happy here, on..." Anisie tried to find the words.

"This is Earth, actually, a planet called Earth."

"Oh," Anisie replied. "I see. This planet, does it look like this all over?" I shook my head. "And these beasts, what are they?"

"Buffalo," I replied, "people got together and saved them from extinction." Anisie nodded. She had heard about things like this happening in her world.

"You, are you happy here?" I again shook my head. "Would you like to go on an adventure... a journey travelling to different worlds?"

I nodded. "I've had enough of this place. I just came

to this park to think about my next move. I'm ready for a change."

"Then, come with me." I agreed and went with Anisie.

We entered black holes and saw shooting stars, planets of burning burgundy and scarlet, the cosmos, solar systems I had never seen before.

"The universe, this world is bigger than you think – stretching far beyond what is familiar to you." We continued the Journey and ended up at Anisie's crystal lair. I gasped.

"You created this? Wow! So cool!"

"Well, we do what we have to do, we all need a home." Anisie showed me her library, tomes that opened up by themselves and talked to the reader, narrating what was on the pages. It was a cool realm where Anisie lived, but I sensed a lot of sadness and a need, a desire, to belong somewhere. Anisie's isolation had made her a wounded bird, a creature with a heart imprisoned by regret, guilt, anger, and alienation.

I sensed this and said, "Could I stay with you awhile? You need the company, and I need a place to go. What do you think?" Anisie nodded. Tears were surfacing, and her eyes were dark with longing.

So, we stayed there, the two outcasts, as I also felt like I didn't belong, all my family having moved away while I stayed for a job in an office; a job that wasn't even that good – I wanted something more, but I just didn't know what. Anisie said quietly, "Seek, and you will find. If you give up, nothing will change." I nodded.

What seemed like weeks later, I was soon ready to go back home to the other world, in the other universe, many universes away, when a Light shone from a rather peculiar-looking figure of a peacock – made out of stained glass. Multi-coloured, it shone like a rainbow. I was entranced.

Anisie was speaking to the peacock. An image of a woman was on the fan of feathers. "Yes, I agree. I will help however I can." For the Queen of the Sand People, Verzini, had helped Anisie before. She told me that she could have been totally transformed into a spider at one point, but the Queen of the Sand People, from the realm of Tucini, pleaded her case. She was successful, and Anisie was able to stay in a human form for at least some of the time, such as when there was a full moon. Anisie would never forget her kindness. Then she asked me if I wanted an escort back to Earth, as there was an urgent matter that she had to attend to, and things would soon have to be put into motion. I said no, I wanted to help Anisie with the task at hand. It seemed like the situation was dire, and I wanted to help this woman, this faerie who had helped me. Anisie nodded with tears in her eyes. She was happy that I was willing to help. She then turned back to the glass peacock and said, "Yes, Verzini, I will help you."

The Queen replied, "The skirmishes, the rebels, it is getting out of control. They do not understand – my future son-in-law is not the enemy – the union of him and my daughter will make the two kingdoms stronger. I will never understand such hatred and ignorance. I will not break this union. Not only is it good for the two realms, my daughter is the happiest she has ever been. I will not relent."

"I understand and agree. I have also made hard choices. Sometimes, these decisions are difficult to make, but once made, you can never go back."

"So, I can count on your support?"

"Always, my Queen, and do you need more supporters, more for your army?"

"If you know of anyone willing to volunteer, let me know. Your support means a lot, Anisie.

"I know you have lost a lot, with what you have done, the choices you have made. But know that I am behind you, all of the way, and this Sister will not let you down." Anisie nodded. The image of the Sand Queen left the mirror. "Are you ready, Selena?"

"Yes."

"Then, it must begin; we leave at dawn tomorrow. If this is what you choose, we must prepare and be at the ready. There are risks. Do you understand?"

"Yes," I said quietly. "I understand. Tell me what to do."

"First, an early sleep, as there is much to do."

I nodded, and a star outside Anisie's window glimmered brightly, as if knowing what was ahead.

***

When we left the next morning, we saw stars, comets, and stardust, swirling around in a whirlpool of amethyst, viridian, carmine, and indigo. Our celestial friends were greeting us while we were on our way, and then we came across a bright ball of Light, flashing bright shades of champagne and amaranthine. As if the tapestry of colour was not enough, we saw something else even more remarkable: a woman surged from a silvery planet, similar to the moon. The planet just appeared out of nowhere, and eyes alight, a siren dressed in armour of metal and seashells, bits of violet and gold conch shells, surged up from the water and threw up an object of silver light. Anisie caught it – a bell of stained glass – which started to emanate multiple colours: viridian, aquamarine, and magenta, and I knew that it reminded her of something. Anisie told me about the Sisters who surged across the sea to the land of druids, the lands of green and mist... and the monastery founded by Saint Fin Barre, founder of Corcaigh... She told me about what they had said: they were talking about a stained glass image – a stained glass image like a rainbow – Saint Fin Barre was robed in sumptuous colours, and looked straight ahead, as if in deep thought. It was his mirror self, his mirror brother, who not only watched over the monastery but the portal to other worlds, including the one of the Snow Queene. This bell reminded Anisie of that.

I had been flying with Anisie, Queen of The Spiders, for what seemed like days, but really, it was only hours. We had stopped at other constellations, other galaxies, and saw stars, saw nebulae where the birth went on of new stars, the Younglings, celestial beings of Light and Sound, New Stars coming out into the world... I gasped at what I was seeing. It was Magic. Anisie nodded at me. Yes, all around them was Magic. Life was magic, no matter where you looked, no matter where you were. Anisie now had the bell. She rang it three times. Then, there was a hush. Then, there was a Hum. A huge Hum.

It reverberated like a sonic boom across the universe. Then, she heard them; I did too – a song, a sing-song of the different stars, galaxies – it was an orchestral wave of Sound. Anisie nodded her head. "This way," she said. "It is time to find out where we are needed." We took off, like a rocket, through the black velvet space dotted with beams of light and currents of sound – a constant, magical, eerie, but comforting hum. We set down on a planet, a world I had never seen before, a planet that Anisie later told me was called Scarentis. Red was everywhere. It was everywhere. Everywhere. She stopped to take stock. She stopped. See... She would See, yes, she Would See. Yes. Yes. Yes.

There were skirmishes up ahead, screams, ear-piercing screams. Anisie and I went closer. Blood was literally spraying all over the ground, making it an ever more sinister red. I was stunned. Anisie held my hand to steady me, as right now, she was in human form because in this world, there was a full moon, or moons, rather. Yes, the glowing pearls were aglow at their full size. Anisie would be in this form for quite some time.

"Come," she said. "Let us see what can be done." We flew into a space, where there was a battle. Creatures, some large, some small. Leopards with wings, dwarves with red, beady eyes, and grass all over their bodies, and hyenawere-wolves, which would momentarily shift back into human form and then become hyenawerewolves again. Tall, long creatures of shadow with light that emanated from their head and back... We saw faeries, warrior faeries, who were the Aziza; faeries who were peaceful usually but would jump into battle if necessary – I had read about them as a kid as I loved fairy tales. On the other side were ninki nankas, creatures in the shape of a dragon with a croco-dile's body, a giraffe's neck, with a head of a horse that had horns. Their bodies were also rainbow-coloured and had blue eyes. There were also more Aziza on the battlefield. The faeries were interspersed; it was quite a mess, trying to fight for good, but Evil was having its way. Evil. Blood continued to run like a river, a large one, coursing through the battlefield that was already crimson. Trees, the cypress, the "trees of life" held dear by the Zukisi, cousin to the Jinn, were also in the fray, sometimes in human form but changing back into tree form. They used their branches to swat at the enemy. Things looked dire. I didn't know what to do. Anisie was also at a loss.

I suddenly piped up, "Anisie, I don't think that we can do anything here. It's too much. Maybe we should leave."

Anisie agreed. "Well, at least we can do this." She closed her eyes and started to hum. "Ummmmmmmm... Ummmmmm... Ummmmmmmmmm..." She continued to hum in long tones, deep, long tones. "Ummmmmmmmmmm... Ummmmmmmm... Ummmmmmmmm..." All the creatures stopped for a moment as if frozen in time. Then, a forcefield went over the entire battlefield, sparkling viridian, aquamarine, magenta, and gold, like the bell of stained glass.

In Gougane Barra, Saint Fin Barre heard the call and also closed his eyes; a rainbow of Light surrounded him, passed through the portal in the monastery, and went through galaxies to Anisie, and she sent it onwards onto the Forcefield Of Light. It would hold. Yes, it would hold. Then, Anisie turned to me. "We have to go, find a way to end this battle. We have to see her again: The Siren, Fercand." I nodded. We were off and then were standing on an ocean surrounded by fire. The same siren, donned in armour of violet and gold, rushed to the surface, appearing in an Orb Of Light.

Anisie said, "Fercand, we seek your assistance. We seek your help. The battle is raging, and something has to be done. We are the key — we know it. We must end it, so we can find The One, and bring her home to Safety. She is the key to everything. I know she is with the Snow Queene, but she cannot stay there forever. She is in sanctuary, I know. For in her world, things are so unbearable that she had to leave. For the heart can only take so much. But she will have to return, for the Story must continue to be written. What can we do? I am... at... a loss..." Anisie's voice broke as she was almost in tears. Destruction for all worlds seemed imminent, but she seemed powerless to stop it. Powerless...

"Don't despair, Sister," said the Siren. "Don't despair. Something can be done. You, as you know, are a collector of stories, being the Spider Queen Of Tiyadima Tinga. You know the importance of the narrative, The Word, spoken and written. You are amassing quite a collection in your library." Anisie nodded her head.

The Siren continued, "Well, I need a book, one that would shed light on why my world is only enshrouded in darkness. We don't see the sun, as you do. Only our moon sends her presence. But there has to be a balance, the dark and the light. My people are dying, for without the Sun, our bodies will eventually turn to dust. Time is running out. We need to find the answer. We need to know. If you find this book and give it to me, I will help you. The Battle will end. But to get this book, you will need three things: fire, a sword, and armour of the finest Elvish silver. Find these three things, and the Book, she will come to you. She will come. Bring her to me, and I will help you in stopping this Battle, so you can find The One. For The One of whom you speak, she is paramount to our world as well. We have heard of The One who sings song, The Lyrical Song that will change all worlds for many generations to come. We have heard of her, connected to Mother —" She stopped and smiled at me.

"The Young One doesn't know. I will leave it at that for now. It is not time yet for her to know the truth, and you, Anisie, I know that you know you're a part of it, but also, for you, it is not time yet to know the full Story. In the meantime, get this book, this tome of Aquamarine Blue, bring her to me, and I will help you."

"Thank you, Sister," said Anisie, quietly. "You don't know how much this means..."

"Yes, I do, and that is why I want to help. We must help each other; we are all part of a chain; we are all connected. Go Forth, I will await your return." The Siren smiled.

"Yes, Sister, I will do so. I will do as you ask. Yes, yes. Thank you." Anisie bowed down to the one in the gleaming armour of silver and conch shells of a dusty rose.

She took my hand, and we disappeared in a cloud of violet dust.

"I have hope," said the Siren simply. "For those who care, want to make a difference, and who want to take a stand, I have hope." She smiled again and jumped back into the water like a silver bullet.

Chapter Two:
It Continues

ANISIE continued flying through the air with me; we settled on a star, one of amaranth and silver. We looked around and walked for a while. Giants of stardust came upon us. They looked at us in surprise, and one made a gesture. "You are Anisie, Queen Of The Spiders. Fercand, the Siren, sent you. Welcome." Anisie nodded. We walked with these tall beings of stardust. Rays of light shone from ahead. We got closer. It was a city, made out of rays of light and orange stardust. They twinkled and glowed. Twinkled and glowed. We went to a castle made out of marble and Elvish silver. The bridge came down; we crossed it, and then we were ushered into the Royal chambers. There was a throne made entirely out of Stardust and bits from Shooting Stars. A woman who was sitting on the throne had eyes of gleaming silver that looked at them deeply, as if in thought.

"You, why are you here?" she asked.

"Well, your people seemed to –" responded Anisie.

"Yes," I know," said the Queen, "but I want to hear it from your lips. So –"

"Well, we are on a quest to find three things: a sword,

armour, and a pit of fire, so we can get the Book, the Tome of Aquamarine. She is the key to ending a war in another world, a planet of red, red, like Death..."

"Yes, I have heard. I understand. My guardsmen will take you there. The sword, it is yours." Anisie thanked her, and on her face, she must have looked surprised as the Queen said, "You thought it would be a battle to get her?" She then laughed. Anisie nodded.

"Well, not in my realm." The Queen laughed. "Life is too short, especially this one... The next...? Well, that is a story for another time. I believe in your cause, and I have heard of her, The One who is the Messenger. She must be protected at all costs, or all our worlds are doomed. Go. I will help you."

We went up the steps of the castle, a long, circular staircase that seemed to go on for miles. Finally, we reached the top. One of the sentinels opened the door. Once inside, it was aglow with the light of a deep forest green. We walked in further. There she was – a sword made out of the finest Elvish silver, curved slightly, with a handle made out of emeralds. I smiled in awe. The sentinels also smiled, and I heard a low laugh.

"The elves, they are good craftsmen," said one Sentinel, with armour of stardust and amethyst. "You. You are lucky to have her. Take care of her and use her wisely." I nodded as well as Anisie. Anisie stepped closer to the glass case that housed the precious sword. She closed her eyes and opened one of her hands. The glass case opened, and the sword flew out, right into her hand. The sentinels all smiled.

"We all wish you well. You must complete this Journey, and bring the book to Queen Fercand, the Siren Queen of the Realm Aquiantis. Things are dire. We have heard of what has happened on the planet Scarentis: the planet of now red soil that is reeking of Death, and will reek of more death, like other worlds, until it is resolved, and the Messenger can go home."

"Yes, I know," said Anisie quietly.

"We all know. And we all wish you well. Here. A gift from us."

Anisie's eyes opened wide in surprise. It was a dagger, a smaller version of the sword, with a ruby handle, and also a pocket watch. "We had found the sword in another world; a world ruled by a king... King Arthur... He was a good king, and wondrous things were to pass. He has gone now to Avalon, but he gave us this upon our visit to him there, when we were accompanying the Queen. They had much to discuss. And the pocket watch... We had found it in another portal by a toadstool. I haven't seen anything like it. Anyway, it's yours, for I know it will have some kind of use, some kind of purpose."

Anisie just nodded. I smiled.

"Youngling," a sentinel spoke. "I am glad you are with Anisie on this Journey. It is good to have a helping hand. Being in solitude is fine, but it is also good to know friendship. We have something for you." A second sentinel, attired the same way as the first, motioned for me to hold out my hand. Instinctively, I closed my eyes. When I opened them, there it was — a star, a star with a million points of Light. "She is a Stargette, one of a long ancestral line. They guide those in need. They are like a compass, but more knowledgeable, more accurate in their readings, and have other gifts. She will help you. Stargettes are assigned from birth to help anyone in need. That is their purpose. You —

she will help you, whenever you are in despair." I nodded; tears started to flood my eyes.

A third sentinel appeared. "Youngling, you will find your purpose. You will find a home. We all need… have a desire to belong. Embrace that. It is nothing to be ashamed of. We all have a need to belong somewhere. You will find it. You will find your path, your home." I continued to nod. In this world, like other worlds I had visited, I was finding my purpose – already – just being with Anisie and accompanying her on her journey. I knew that I would find my place. Yes, a place where I belonged.

The sentinels all smiled. We thanked them and descended down the circular staircase, not saying a word. It was good. It was very good. We were on our way. The world that we saw, enshrouded in red and reeking of Death, she had a chance. So, too, did the Messenger, as she could continue to be protected, enabling her to continue on her path, to be what she was meant to be, to save all worlds, yes, to save all worlds.

Anisie and I were travelling again – taking flight – after thanking the Queen of Silver. The sentinels took us to a ship, where we sailed, swimming through oceans of Night, with only the stars to guide us. The Stargette rose into the air after I let her go from my hand, and the Stargette would venture forth, here and there, ahead of the ship, to scout and look for danger, as well as the way to our next destination, to find the next piece, the next object, that would lead us to the Tome of Aquamarine.

We came to a planet, one with many rings; Anisie had heard of her, and I definitely had. It was Saturn. The ship of oak with sails of silver spun by stargettes and elves started billowing from currents of cosmic air. We got closer to Saturn. The ship touched one of the rings – it took us deeper into the planet's lair. I had read about the poisonous gases and so on. I knew since Anisie was immortal, she would always be protected, but I also knew she would make sure that I was protected as well. We continued closer, sailing into the realm, coming closer, and closer… Then, we heard a thud, then a big Bump.

Bats ascending from a magenta atmosphere, bats with pieces of the multicoloured rings of Saturn, as well as magenta stardust, flew out at us. We were being attacked. There were also elves with dark green eyes and sharp claws, who came at us, one even scratching my shoulder. Anisie quickly healed it, and then, quietly said a few words – a bubble of Light, indigo, viridian, and persimmon, surrounded us. But it was only for a moment, as the stench of Evil was so strong, so strong…Yes, Yes, YES.

Then, once the bubble disappeared, I started to hum like Anisie, and a sword with an emerald handle appeared in my hand, and armour of the finest Elvish silver was on my body. I rose up and started to fight the bats of magenta dust and bits of the rings of Saturn. I chopped heads off, and the same with the elves of fangs and long claws. Anisie did the same. Since Saturn had many moons, and they were all full, Anisie was still in human form. As she closed her eyes, the Adinkra symbols on her dress became maces, attacking and killing the creatures. Some of the other symbols turned into daggers and killed the other creatures instantly. Her dress, made out of crystal silk, became aglow and emanated a bright fire – balls of fire, shining gold and carmine, burst off and killed more of the beasts. These balls of fire quickly turned round and round like a whirling dervish, killing more creatures left and right. I had never seen anything like it. I was mystified and entranced, and the only word that came out of my mouth was "Cool." Anisie smiled. Then, once all the creatures fell from the sky to their deaths, if they were not dead already, Anisie and I shot forth like arrows and reappeared on the ship.

The stargette created a silver aura around us with her stardust, and we continued. We saw a hole, a black hole, and went through it. It was very unstable, huge blasts of winds and millions of red eyes were there to greet us, and shadows of beasts – some hyenawerewolves, some leopards with wings – started to growl at us. Anisie closed her eyes and surrounded us with a bubble of Light. The stargette went ahead to see what other dangers lurked.

Then, we saw another door – yes, another door – and we went inside. Another battle was raging: chimeras, sphinxes, ninki nankas, and so on. Anisie and I had no idea what was going on. We got closer. More blood was being spilled, and it did not bode well. We flew in, we two women, undetected as the bubble of Light made us invisible. We got closer and closer, closer and closer.

Then, there it was – a pit of fire that could be seen for miles. Yes, I thought, one of the things we needed for the Siren Queen. We homed in, but then, "Halt!" said a voice. "Who are you? Identify yourself. Go no further!" It was an Aziza faerie, a guide to hunters if they were ever lost or in need of assistance. The one Aziza was dressed in burgundy, with a sword and shield. "We are the guardians of this fire. It is a beacon to ones who are lost. There is a battle brewing, but we are the ones who have chosen to stay behind to protect her. Who are you?"

"I am Anisie, Queen of the Spider World, and here is... another Sister from another world."

The faerie looked at me. She smiled. "You are from Earth. We know of your kind. We know why you are here. Welcome, but I wish it were under better circumstances. Anisie, things do not look good. I don't know... the battle, we are losing, all will be lost, and the fire..."

"Don't give up, Sister. We are here to help. We will help you, and we are also on the lookout for armour, but Selena is already donning –"

"No, that is not the one," said the faerie, smiling. "It is a fine piece of metalwork, but that is not the one. You are also looking for a torch of fire," added the Aziza.

"Yes, is this...?" Anisie pointed toward the tall flame.

"No," said the faerie. "But there is another. We can take you to Her. Help us with this battle, and we will take you to Her."

"Agreed," sighed Anisie in relief. "Agreed. What do we do?"

The faerie and Anisie went aside and discussed battle strategies. Anisie nodded. She then walked back to me. Anisie said, very decisively, "Selena, this is what has to be done." I nodded after what she had told me to do.

The Aziza created a bubble Of Light around the tall Flame Of Fire, Protector of hunters, and anyone else in need, and a Light for those who stayed behind. Anisie, the stargette, and I did the same, surrounding ourselves with a bubble of Light. Then, we went out onto the battlefield, descending into chaos.

The bubble disappeared, but then I sprang into action – jujitsu and karate surged through my veins, as I began killing many beasts. Anisie did the same, and the stargette, she shimmered many colours, blinding many of the evil creatures, so we could kill them quickly.

The stargette could also shoot balls of Fire and deadly stardust – rising up, spinning around quickly like Anisie, killing many. We and the shining constellation of light, the Stargette, continued forward, forging a path of Strength and Fury. We continued.

More beasts of magenta stardust, like bats, more hyenawerewolves, and shadows emanating a strange light from their heads and backs, came forth; they were immediately struck down. Lions, leopards with wings, blue eagles with big claws flying around the air – also struck dead. We went to the top of the mountain, and there was another beast, a bear that was also part giant and part demon. He had thick horns on his head and eyes that gleamed red like Death.

Anisie went forward, surging in strength and speed, as a dagger appeared in her hand. She threw it and hit the beast in his eye. She threw another, and it hit the beast in the other eye. She quickly took a sword and chopped off both his hands, before a bow and arrow magically appeared in her hand. She took a shot, when, out of nowhere, a bat who was not quite dead took a swipe at Anisie. She screamed. I saw what happened and quickly flew to her aid. I took Anisie out of the air and laid her on the ground.

The stargette twinkled at me to continue the fight, before it turned towards Anisie, beaming healing rays of Light into the wounded woman. In the meantime, I, in armour of the finest silver, now flying back up into the air, took one look at the Beast and screamed, "Noooooooooooooo... Noooooooooooooo..." I screamed those words and looked at the beast, her chestnut eyes aflame: suddenly, a shield had appeared, made out of the finest stardust and the breath of the moon, and then I also had a long sword – it was the sword of the Tuatha Dé Danann, and I threw it at the

Beast. I held the shield in front of my body – in one moment, there was a large "Kabbbbboooooooooooooooom...." and the Beast was dead.

There were large cries of delight and Victory from down below. Even the creatures of Evil who saw, had appreciation and respect in their eyes. They knew that this one – this young one – was a fine warrior, not to be messed with. The beings of Evil disappeared. I descended to the ground below to see how Anisie was doing. "Will she be all right?" I asked the Stargette.

She twinkled, "Yes." I descended further, my feet finally touching the ground. The stargette continued to look at me. Stargette couldn't speak but twinkled her responses, and she would send out feelings or emotions, so you knew exactly what she was saying or thinking. I then knew Anisie would be all right. One of the Aziza looked at Anisie. Another stood by with a smile on her face.

"She will be all right," they said together. "She will be all right."

"Come back to the Flame," said the one wearing a wrap of burgundy around her. "Odae wants to talk to you." She pointed to a tall woman wearing a wrap of magenta around her. I walked up to Odae, as Anisie had to rest, and the stargette stayed by her side.

"Selena," said the Aziza named Odae, their leader, the Queen of this planet called Ariendes. "You have done well. You are a warrior. We all knew what you were capable of. Now, quickly, we must hurry; we cannot wait. We have to find her, the Sister of this Fire, the one you must take to Fercand, Queen of the Sirens." I nodded.

We walked through a forest of light and sound: there were trees of stardust that twinkled, but there were also cypress trees and even oak, as these trees of Life had many lives and many homes.

"Yes, many things have more than one home – remember that, Selena. For us, we have more than one." I nodded. We continued further into the Forest. There were hyenas with golden wings, lions with the same, and wombats; they looked up. The Aziza continued, "They are the Mystical ones: they have Sisters and Brothers down on Earth, as you know." I nodded. We continued forth. There, in the middle of the clearing, was a fire – not as large as the other, but a beautiful flame of vermilion, azure, and gold, with the azure, bordering on an aquamarine, burning bright in the centre. "Yes, there she is. Keeper of all secrets, protector of all worlds. You can take her." I looked hesitant.

"It's all right. The Siren Queen requested her presence, and so it will be so. So, it will be. Take her." I nodded, took a deep breath, and walked forward. I didn't know what to do, but instantly, I held out my hands and instinctively started to hum like I did earlier. Then, it happened. It got dark suddenly, the Wind picked up, and there were swirls of Light – a circle, circling faster and faster, like a black hole. I continued to hum and wasn't afraid because I knew, in my heart, I didn't have to be.

I continued to hum; the fire lifted, circled in on my own axis, and then disappeared into a glass flask studded with diamonds that suddenly appeared in my hand. Then, a cork of emeralds and rubies appeared and closed the flask. The Light returned to the clearing with the stars twinkling above.

"You have done it," said the Aziza. "Yes, you are the one, Warrior and Sister to us all. I am honoured to have met you, Selena. Yes, you will always have a home with us. You will always belong somewhere, and you will always have a home with us. Stay whenever you like." My eyes were brimming with happiness; I had never felt like this before. I had found a home – there would be others, but this was my first. I belonged somewhere, because for all of us, immortal or human, mystical or not, we had to belong somewhere. We all had to belong. I hugged her, swimming in joy.

"Go forth, Sister," said Odae, smiling. "We are with you. You will look after Anisie. I know you will. It is not easy for her, the decision she had made to defy King Jobali. She will tell you her story, her entire story, when it is time. But we have all made decisions – some good, some that haunt us – but we have to move on and do the best we can, for these decisions cannot be undone. I know you understand. Go to her. She will be ready. The stargette has healed her. You are ready too."

"Thank you." I smiled at this Aziza who was now wrapped in emerald and fuchsia.

"It is Odae," she said, as if she knew what I was thinking. "That is my name. Go forth, Sister. I will see you again. If not in this lifetime, the next. Go forth and be well." I nodded again and went back to where Anisie lay.

Her eyes were open, and she did look a lot better. Her skin didn't look so pale, and her eyes were no longer red. The sweat had disappeared from her brow.

"Anisie, Sister," I added, "we have to go now."

"Yes, Selena," replied Anisie, slowly but surely. "And… congratulations. You are one of us now. You always were, you just didn't know it. Your home is with us, no matter where you go. And you are always welcome to return. We will welcome you with open arms. Yes, with open arms.

This is home – for all of us." I knew what she meant, for it was with ones who cared about you, no matter where they were, that was home. I knew now. And I had found my purpose. That was important too, to have a purpose. My eyes were drowning in tears. It was a glorious day. The stargette started to gleam and shine, gleam and shine; she even started to make beeping noises. "She's saying it's time to go," said Anisie. "You are right, Selena, we must leave now – there is much more ahead of us."

Anisie got up slowly as she was still recovering, and the stargette summoned the ship. The ship descended, ready, and since the ship was also a mystical being, she could repair herself, and she looked just like new, as if she had never been at war.

"Let's go, Zoydae." Anisie already knew the ship's name. "Let's go forth, for now we need just one more piece of the puzzle. Let us go, Now." I agreed, nodding, and the stargette twinkled in response. We stepped onto the ship, with its fine bow of amaranth crystal, and jetted off into the ocean of Night, sails billowing, creating an aerial music. We were on the next journey, to find her, the suit of armour, similar to what I had but even more glorious. We continued to sail through galaxies, seeing shooting stars, stars like the ones from Stargette's realm, and other constellations – so many things. I enjoyed this time and these adventures. I had found my calling. Could I ever go back to the way I was? I wasn't sure. Anyway, I wouldn't think about that now. I had to think about the task at hand – finding the suit of armour.

Chapter Three:
Beginnings

S TARGETTE started to twinkle; she saw a beacon, a flashing beacon. She gestured with one of her arms, one of her many arms of Light, being a Star, and Anisie nodded in response. The ship sped faster toward the beacon. Once we got to the planet, the ship touched down. Anisie got off the ship first.

"Wait," she said to me. "Let's just see what is here – I will go first to see... To seek. Stay for now. Stargette, come with me." Stargette created an orb of light that surrounded the ship and me to keep us safe. This planet was dark and dank, murky, with no Light. Stargette was a star from the celestial line of stargettes, so Anisie wouldn't have any problem having Stargette as a guide. The two continued. Mists surrounded them. They seemed to clear, but it was not easy to see ahead.

Stargette multiplied into three stars to help show the way. Anisie smiled, thanking the Celestial Being. They continued. Anisie's feet sensed water, so she closed her eyes and conjured up a small rowboat, and she paddled, steering the boat through the water. Stargette went ahead to see what was there and give Anisie another source of light.

Anisie continued to paddle the boat. Then, they saw an island. They went closer. I was looking through a hand-held telescope, an Ovienne, as told to me by Anisie – you could see things from very far away as if they were in front of you. The telescope shimmered like diamonds and was made out of the finest steel, forged by the breath of a dragon.

There was a small island, and on that island, something shimmered. Anisie paddled the boat closer to the island and docked. She walked carefully toward the shining object. Stargette was just before her and, as a precaution, created a wall of Light before and around them for protection. Anisie agreed that it was the right move. They went closer. It was armour – with seaweed, moss, and rust on it. It didn't look anything like the treasure that Fercand mentioned. Anisie got closer. I thought that it looked useless, seeing it through the telescope. Why were we taken here? Well, what do we do? I thought. I then decided, and I knew Anisie would agree, that this is what we have to take back. I saw Anisie reach out to touch the suit of armour, when a bright orb of Light appeared, and then, more than one. A whole row of golden orbs descended, and then, one by one, they became human beings. Well, what looked like human beings.

"Yes, Anisie. Welcome. We are –" I heard everything as this magical telescope was like a microphone and I could hear any conversation, any word spoken.

Anisie replied, "Yes, you are the ones from across the seas that settled the island of green and mist.... home to the druids, Gougane Barra, Saint Fin Barre. You..."

"Yes," they said, "we are the Tuatha Dé Dannan. We are they. Welcome, we have wanted to meet you for a long time, but the time was not right. We, the Mystical Ones, we know of another people from the land of pyramids, desert, The Sphinx – they also went to this land, our land, and so there are also those with swarthy features, also part of the Celtic line. This is a land of many peoples, of Vikings, and so on. For some, the water is in their blood – seamen sailing the ships, women as warriors, the Vikings but also – yes, we remember, I remember. Yes. I know you do. I know you do. Our worlds are in trouble, Anisie. Soon, we have to go underground, for there are others who will take our home. But until that happens, we can appear to you and help you, so we are here. You are in need of something."

"Yes… armour, this suit of armour. But look… she has seen better days."

"Yes, Anisie." A tall woman came forward. She was a goddess with eyes of flaming amaranthine. "Yes, she has seen better days, but whatever has come to pass will come again and be anew. Touch her again, Anisie."

Anisie did, and she gasped. Lights in multiplicity surrounded the armour, and so did an orb of bright violet, and lifted the suit of armour into the air – she started to transform. She then became gold and silver, with mother-of-pearl adorning her. Emblazoned on her chest were symbols: one was a dragon, the other, she couldn't quite see. The helmet, again gold and silver, was decorated with beads of amethyst and shiny, golden mother-of-pearl. The dragon symbol was emblazoned on it, too – the piece that would shield the face. Anisie hadn't seen anything like it. Anything was possible.

"Anisie, we leave her in your charge," said the same tall goddess, with hair of a bright scarlet and eyes changing to a darker reddish purple. Later, Anisie would discover that she was talking to Brigid, the passionate goddess of poetry, the Protector Of Storytellers, Bards, all those who crafted Stories from The Word.

The tall woman continued, "We know of the Battle, and of another yet to come. The Messenger, she must be protected at all costs. We, the Tuatha Dé Dannan, are here to help in that fight. We will do all that we can before we must go to the world below for our safety. In the meantime, take this as our gift. We are so honoured to have met you, and for that, we have another gift. Close your eyes." Anisie closed them. All the Celtic gods and goddesses came together, emanating heliotrope, saffron, and rose from their velvet and silk robes. Druids suddenly appeared, some with faces of an almond or cocoa hue, and cloaked in black, scarlet, or azure; they all walked closer and held hands. Altogether, the Mystical Ones, along with their cloaked counterparts, who were stewards of magic, started to chant – not unlike Anisie – in musical tones, Celtic songs. To Anisie, they sounded a bit like the Egyptian songs she had heard before… Was there a connection?

She heard the voice of a druid who had a beautiful almond tone to her skin. She told Anisie telepathically, "Yes, there is a connection – through time and space, through shared hearts…" Anisie just smiled, and so did Brigid, who also heard the conversation, having telepathic abilities, being a goddess. The tall woman with bright scarlet hair just looked at Anisie with a smile on her face. The Celtic gods and goddesses, as well as all the druids, continued to chant and sing. Chant and sing.

Then, something miraculous happened: a bright ray of light surrounded Anisie. What surrounded her were multiple layers of Light, of a piercing cerulean, mauve, persimmon, a haunting forest green, and a beautiful, bountiful gold. Over and over again, they sang – yes, they sang – poetry amongst the humming, and the words, which were a music that reached the ears, a sonic, a lyric, a sonic. Yes, yes, yes, and yes – they sang, they sang, and they sang. And then something glass-like tumbled out from Anisie's body and burst into pieces, but since Anisie was surrounded by layers of Light, she was protected.

She opened her eyes, and there was the body of a large spider, reddish black, looking at her. She looked at the gods and goddesses.

"Anisie, you have suffered enough. You asked to be treated with dignity and respect, and what that king did was uncalled for. You deserved better. We are sorry for how you were treated. It was an injustice. We make amends. We lift you up, in story and song, song and story. May you be who you always were, who you are now. You are free to be whoever you are meant to be. Not to be trapped, but to have a choice. We all need choices. We all need choices and second chances. Regret is a hard thing to bear. But not to be given a second chance, especially one who is so deserving – that is injustice. Stand up, Anisie, and rise."

She did, and her body started to rise off the ground. "You are one of us, being a Mystical One from the realm; for all worlds are connected, and we are all One. Go Forth, Anisie, now you have the armour, the pyre of fire, and the sword. Go forth to the Siren Queen. As another gift, we give you this –" Anisie's eyes lit up with surprise: it was the tome, the tome of Aquamarine. The goddess, Brigid, continued, "It is the key to all things. It is the key to the past, present, and future. Take it to her, the Siren, queen of that world. They are in need of Light. For it is not good for a world to be surrounded entirely and permanently only by darkness. There must always be a balance: light and dark. And there, there is no balance. Go Forth, Anisie. Go forth. We are all behind you. You will do well; you are already, and you will find the Messenger. For soon, it is time to bring her Home to continue the Story. You, Anisie, you are a beloved, beloved Sister. Do not forget. Do not forget. Whenever you are in trouble and despair, think of us – we will always come to your aid, even when we have to descend to the world beneath. Yes, You, my child. Go forth, for you know your purpose and know that you belong." Anisie smiled and looked at her hands and legs. She still couldn't believe it.

"That will not change, Dear One. We are not ones to trifle with people's lives, people's hearts. That is the will of Others. But not us. We will keep our Word. You are Free. For you were willing to risk your life for others. That is more than commendable. That bravery, that strength will be desperately needed to save all our worlds. You are one Of Us. You are an honoured member of the Tuatha Dé Dannan... You will meet others, that we know. The one who guards over...the Patron Saint of Corcaigh, you will meet him soon enough. Go forth, Child, know that you are not alone. You are not alone."

Anisie smiled, and her body slowly descended to the ground. The Celtic gods and goddesses, the Tuatha Dé Dannan, as well as the druids, who seemed to be of a celestial nature and were also a part of the Tuatha Dé Dannan, disappeared. The circle was complete. Anisie went back, with Stargette carrying the beautiful suit of armour to the ship where I waited. Swimming through the universe, floating through oceans of black velvet punctuated by stars, we smiled, and the stargette sparkled gold and silver, then, beryl, vermilion, and mauve. Then, persimmon, viridian, and gold. Yes, Yes, a Journey had ended, but another had Begun. We all went to the Siren Queen and gave her the four items: the pyre of fire in a glass flask, the sword, the beautiful suit of armour unforgettably decorated with mother-of-pearl and amethysts, and the Book of Aquamarine.

The Siren was pleased, also knowing that we stopped the battle in two worlds: Scarentis, the red planet, and on the planet Ariendes, home to the Aziza, led by their kind but fierce leader, Odae.

"You three have done well. Yes, you have done well." All four items floated to the Siren, and the Book of Aquamarine, a memorable tome of blue like the ocean, opened up as if instinctively, and then she started to speak of worlds, of stories.

Then the book said, "The Messenger – she has to embark on more adventures. Two more, and then she has to go back to her world – temporarily. Before that, other worlds await, and afterwards, she must set forth to an island surrounded by blue, another island of story, an island of opportunity. There, her journey must continue, and there, that journey will end. She must discover more about who she is. She must… and for the latter part of that journey, she must go alone. You three will join Others, other Sisters, to help the One fulfill her final quest. Yes, this is how it will be, how it was written, and fate must reveal herself. Yes, you will be meeting others. For if the Messenger does not fulfill her final quest, all worlds are in jeopardy, all in danger of being immersed in eternal darkness. No Reams of Light. Nothing. For there must always be a balance, and with Eternal Darkness…" The book, called Shericantaes, trailed off.

The Siren Queen shivered. "I don't know quite what to make of it, of what the book speaks. But what I do know is this – Time is at a premium. You must Go… NOW. You, you three, you will meet the other Sisters."

The siren looked at her guardsmen. A sentinel spoke in response, "Maybe we can accompany Anisie, Selena, and the stargette." The Queen nodded.

"Sentinel, I think it is a good idea. Accompany these women – accompany them and help them on this journey. You must. It is time. But first, rest is needed. It will be an arduous, long Journey. Rest. You all must be At The Ready." Everyone nodded. The book suddenly disappeared, but the other items remained.

The Siren again spoke. "The suit of armour, the fire, the sword, they are all for you, Anisie. I know that the Tuatha Dé Dannan talked to you. They are pleased. I know they have gifted you back your true immortal self, as that is what you deserved. Those in despair need not stay despondent. That is not our way. Rest, for the journey, the next one, will indeed be difficult. The book is in my study, in the turret. I will consult with her later. For now, everyone must rest. I'll retire a bit later, after I have consulted with Shericantaes." The Siren Queen, Fercand, spoke those words firmly and with purpose. She continued, "Take these guests to the chambers."

"Yes, my Queen," said one of the ladies-in-waiting, wrapped in a leaf of lily. "It will be done."

"Yes, I must attend to things. A good night to all and sweet dreams. You all deserve a bountiful rest tonight." The lady-in-waiting took Anisie, me, and Stargette to our chambers.

I noticed that Stargette was a bit hesitant, staying behind.

"No, Stargette," said Queen Fercand. "You have done well. You rest. You must be a beacon for these two. The journey will be very rough. They will need a beacon – not just a compass, but a knowledgeable guiding force. You must be there for them no matter what the cost. You must be ready." The stargette twinkled in response. "I know you would understand. Good night, dear one." Stargette twinkled again.

Anisie told me later that, after the Siren Queen left us, she ascended up into her study in the turret where the book was waiting for her. Many symbols awaited the Queen, but some she didn't know; they were from the Adinkra language, the language of the Ashanti. Queen Fercand knew she had a Sister knowledgeable about this beautiful symbolic language. The Sister appeared in robes of ebony and maroon, filled with many Adinkra symbols. They read the book together, and they both nodded. They both then closed their eyes and held hands. Suddenly, reams of Light surrounded the planet, pierced the seas of darkness, the seas of black, and suddenly it was day, for that planet had not seen daylight in decades. Anisie saw in her mind's eye what was happening, as she had that gift, and the Queen had more questions for her that night after Anisie entered her bedchamber. The Queen also wanted her guest, the faerie Sharcaend, to talk to Anisie as well. After much discussion about the Adinkra language and so on, Anisie, the Queen, and her guest saw that suddenly there was a sun, and clouds – streams of clouds. The three couldn't believe it, especially the Siren Queen, who cried.

"I never thought –" she whispered.

"Dear Sister," said Sharcaend, with beautiful mocha skin, a dress made of crystal silk, and robes of ebony and maroon. "Anything is possible. We are here to help each other. When we do that, yes, anything is possible." She gave the Queen a big hug and also hugged Anisie, who had joined them for this Mystical Moment that none of them thought they would see in this lifetime.

Chapter Four:
To See The One

ANISIE, Stargette, and I left the castle in the morning, greeted by a beautiful dawn. The Queen still marvelled at what happened – the miracle, the experience – and was waiting for it to end. But it had not. Eternal night had disappeared, and the day was back, filled with sunshine, golden sunshine.

The Queen was enraptured, and so were the Sentinels and the rest of the people in the realm of Aquiantis. Some of the sentinels decided to go with the three, even though it could mean Death, but they believed in the cause so much. They also believed in meeting and protecting the Messenger, and they were determined to see it all through. So, we all left in the ship, sails billowing for another world, another world to meet this Messenger. It took us again through different worlds, black holes, with stars as our guide, and the ever-faithful Stargette charged with our safety.

We traversed different worlds, went through various galaxies – Andromeda, the Milky Way – when we happened upon another Black Hole; we went through, and then saw a land of green and mist, and some mountains in the background. There was a monastery almost surrounded by water. It was quiet; the silence only broken by the chirping of birds. A man appeared before them in robes of carmine, gold, and azure. He smiled, his dark brown eyes gleaming.

"Come," he said. "Come." We walked toward the monastery, nestled in this majestic hideaway. We saw his mirror brother in the stained glass. He gestured toward it, and we sauntered through. That gentle guide I later found out was Saint Fin Barre.

Then, there were oceans of Night, black, then a bright flood of stars, some cousins to Stargette, and she twinkled at them happily. They twinkled back, and we continued moving forward until we came across a plain of ice and snow. We got closer. Then, a castle appeared in the distance. We continued. Saint Fin Barre, who was the Patron Saint of Corcaigh, ushered us on. "You will be safe," he said. We continued. A bridge lowered, and they crossed it. We went up a steep circular staircase, escorted by faeries dressed in robes of ice and crystal, and muffs. Their hair was a white silver, and some eyes gleamed cobalt, others violet. We continued up the stairs.

Once we reached a door of bright magenta, it opened, and there she was – the Snow Queene – bejewelled with crystal, diamonds, and rubies, a robe of crystal silk, and a twinkling muff with mother-of-pearl. She had a scarlet cap on her head with a fringe of white fur. She smiled from her throne of emeralds and rubies.

"Welcome," she said. "I know who you would like to have an audience with. Come with me." She got up from her throne and walked to another chamber in a turret, not dissimilar to the Queen Siren's turret. She opened the door of crystal, and there she was – quill in hand at a desk of marble and quartz. She turned around, dressed in silver trimmed with white fur and an evergreen cap stitched with crystal thread. Her cape over the dress was scarlet, and she looked becoming – the scarlet a compliment to her beautiful mocha skin. Her eyes glimmered a bright brown, like a bright chestnut.

"Welcome," she said. "I am happy to meet you all." A sentinel rushed forward and immediately went down on one knee.

"I am honoured to meet you. You are she. You are the Messenger, Singer of Songs, and the great-great-great-granddaughter of Mother Mnemosyne, Mother Of The Ten Muses. I never thought I would see the day. I am forever at your service."

"Rise," said Harriet E. Wilson, smiling warmly. "I am honoured. Yes, I am honoured. Rise. Such pomp and circumstance – that is not me. But I thank you. There is much to do. I am writing what I think will be one of my best works. I will have to get it out into the world, somehow. I am going between two worlds: this one and the other. But for now, I need a reprieve. At this time, being me – a woman of colour – is not easy. I need an oasis of calm, and I have it here. I have found out that Mother Mnemosyne is my great-great-great-grandmother. It makes a lot of sense as she always talks to me, as well as her daughters, especially the Muse of Poetry. But there was another, a twin Sister, another Muse of Poetry, but also a Goddess of Justice. Her name is Tuerini. She is not talked about, for some reason, but maybe – somehow – I will later know why. The Snow Queene tells me I must go on a journey to know more about who I am. Will you, Sentinel, and all that the Siren Queen has commanded, help me on this quest?" They all nodded.

Anisie stepped forth with me by her side. "It's also an honour for me to meet you," said Anisie quietly. "I also thought I would never see the day."

"Me, as well," I laughed. "A girlfriend gave me an emerald volume of your poetry –unusual, as it looked like a journal – and your poem, 'Fading Away' was in there. It helped me to see that I was not alone – that many experience despair, darkness, and frustration. I'm sure that you are working on other things now. It was meant to be, me meeting you."

Harriet had tears come to her eyes. "Well, that is good to hear. I have known for quite some time that it is not all I will write, and what I am working on – it is coming quickly. I have written other poems that were not published, but I am proud of that one. The genesis, it came..." More tears came to her eyes.

"It came from a dark place, I am sure," I said quietly and nodded. Somehow, by looking at my newfound Sister, Anisie, I knew that she knew much more than she could ever tell me. There would be more adventures, more challenges to come. Anisie also knew that because we were also travelling through different planes of Time, Harriet would later know about the rest of her work that would go into the world – soon enough – it would only be a matter of time. I was told that another group would soon enter the castle: a group that also had connections with this author. I was intrigued and looked forward to learning more.

There was a celebration with food and drink for all. Many people from the Snow Queene's realm appeared, including Saint Fin Barre, Patron Saint Of Corcaigh. Druids also came out and discussed things with the sentinels and with Anisie, as she was also a collector of stories that she amassed in her library. She wanted to know more about the Druid folklore, especially the folklore around the oak tree, their Tree Of Life. She knew of another people, the Jinn, where the cypress tree was their Tree Of Life. So many connections, similarities, so many revelations. Yes, there was much to discuss. The Snow Queene was happy.

Harriet gave a reading of her finished poems, as those she was still working on she was not ready to share yet. But no one minded; they were just happy to hear her voice, raised in song – the lyric song – and Anisie smiled, for more was to come for Harriet. Yes, the work she was focussing on and spending time with, Anisie knew, would change the world – not in the way Harriet would think, but still, it would have an everlasting impact and would forever leave an indelible imprint on the human psyche.

Harriet was the great-great-great-granddaughter of Mother Mnemosyne, and the great-great-granddaughter of the twin sister, Tuerini, who was not only the Muse of Poetry but also the Goddess of Justice. She would have been proud of her great-great-granddaughter, Harriet. Yes, Tuerini would have been proud. And her daughter? Yes, Dhakirah, the mystical daughter of Tuerini and now a member of the Ashanti tribe, also great-grandmother to Harriet, would have been very proud as well. Dhakirah was up in the heavens, looking down. She was proud of her girl, her daughter, Boahinmaa. She had always known that Boahinmaa had the gift – the Gift of Memory – as well as foresight and storytelling. Dhakirah was honoured to be Boahinmaa's mother. Dhakirah had always known that she and Boahinmaa were from a different place, a different time, but the Ashanti tribe accepted both of them anyway. When a man with a long silver beard appeared before the tribe, they knew that any offspring that Dhakirah would have when she was grown would be special.

They knew that Dhakirah had a purpose, and that any of her offspring would have a purpose, too – more than one – as all people did, whether mortal or immortal. The tribe, from the ancestral line of the Ashanti, was honoured to help. And when Dhakirah gave birth to her daughter, Boahinmaa, she knew she was part of a chain – a connection, a celestial connection – that would make the world a better place. She didn't know how, but somehow, she knew that Boahinmaa was a part of it; yes, she was the Key. The key to it all. And she was happy to see her daughter, Boahinmaa, fulfilling her purpose – her Destiny – being a Singer Of Song, creating a lyric music, and the same with her granddaughter, who would also follow Boahinmaa on that path. Boahinmaa's granddaughter, Harriet E. Wilson, who would also be a Singer Of Song.

***

Chrysalis: a weave of ice and snow. She lurched, eyes bright. She appeared ghastly but beautiful in shades of pale blue.

"Come," she said, "Come... it is –"

Mirrors of ice surrounded her. They played and played; they danced and played. I heard a voice, "Harriet! Remember, Harriet –"

And then there was a glint in her eye. "Come with me –" she whispered. "COME WITH ME. The Power and the Glory; The Power And The Glory –"

She murmured, murmured in hollow gasps, songs of stillness in the air, like Frost or like a gourd that was frozen and now getting warm in the sun.

I was dreaming. I was dreaming.

"Once, there was..." And once again, I was in the midst of Dreamland. Yes, it was… Time… To… Dream…

41

Chapter Five:
Harriet: The Meeting

SWIRLING around in bursts of air, the woman with blue skin but wispy emerald eyes looked at me, eyes glistening, with an aura of maroon, cerulean, and emerald surrounding her hand.

"What?" I gasped.

"Shhh... No one must know. The Cargines are after us – after me! There are not many of us left, and we are hunted. To heal is my gift; to heal is my curse, for if I refuse, a light – an aura of colour – surrounds my left hand. For us, the Harvandis, we all heal. Our healing gifts are in our left hands. Yes... I am Shareena. Yes... And you – You have mysteries, you have gifts. Your name – It's coming, but only slowly sifting into my mind... I just Can't..."

"Harriet," I whispered. "In my dreams, I come here, at night, and even sometimes during the day when time allows. My waking dreams –when I put them onto paper, it's a record of where I have been. I am remembering... a woman, tall with fiery blue eyes and jet-black hair, and young women surrounding her... I am remembering. What does it all mean? Maybe you can tell me. Sometimes, I think I know, but other times... It's still a puzzle, and I am trying

To Figure It Out..."

"Yes, Harriet, you are trying to figure it out, to understand it all, because you dare to Remember... Yes, child, you are remembering. There is a book in the possession of the ones from across the sea, those who went to the land of green and mist, resided over by ancient ones such as Saint Fin Barre, and whose totems are the trees, the Wise Ones, the Oak. Yes, Yes – They also knew about you... The Celts. Because of Story, they are fierce storytellers – especially one, Brigid. She knew about you... Yes, Harriet, she had already known about you, for they have powers beyond explanation, including foresight. Yes, they already knew of you." I must have looked surprised, because she then smiled. "It will all make sense in time. You will see. It will all make sense in time. The Harvandis – we remember, we remember the Dreams, the lands of cloud and mist give clarity, even to those memories from waking dreams – the ones you follow as your feet touch the ground, and you see the rising sun, not just the ones you experience at night, asleep in your bedclothes."

I nodded. She understood. Yes, she understood.

"It will all come to pass; why you are here, Harriet, why you are here with us. Yes, it will all be revealed in time."

I nodded again. I not only felt a sense of peace, but a sense of purpose, finally knowing my role in this universe. After leaving home because my father died, being ripped from everything I knew, to stay with people who treated me so horribly. My mother did the best she could but knew, at the same time, that she could not take care of me by herself. Sometimes, to do the right thing is the most difficult thing you will ever have to do. Sometimes, there are no choices.

My mother – I loved her. I know it wasn't easy being connected to and in love with my father – a hard-working man, a cooper, but he had a mahogany tone in his skin. That is what they saw… white folks. So many awkward glances, so many pauses, pregnant with disbelief, ignorance, and no understanding that love is just love, and that's all it is. We are made to love. Yes, there are so many who do not understand that. So many. Mama – Yes, I know it was hard for her, and maybe it was a relief for her to give me up. Maybe it was a relief, but I don't blame her. She is my mother, and not only that – she did The Best She Could. A white woman in a world that did not accept her husband or child – people with an ebony or mahogany tone. They do not accept us, and I don't know when they ever will. I write my words so that I can save my boy not just from poverty but from impending death. I hope that I can make it in time. I can only do my best.

I wish my mother was still with me. I remember the words she sang to me, especially the Irish songs she would often sing.

> My Bonnie lies over the ocean,
> My Bonnie lies over the sea,
> My Bonnie lies over the ocean,
> So, bring back my Bonnie to me.

Those words would echo and reverberate. Echo and reverberate.

And Shareena said, "You are Remembering. The Irish – it is a part of you. Don't forget. It is a part of you, and that song, it will lyricize, materialize in words. You are writing a novel, a novel to free your boy. A novel. You must finish it."

"Will it save him… my boy?"

Shareena hesitated and then said, "You can only do your best in this world. I cannot say what will happen or what will materialize. I am not a soothsayer in that way; A foreteller of fate. You must wait, and then you will know. Wait and know. Wait and know. Yes. Wait and know. No matter what happens, remember that everything happens for a reason. Remember that and then let go. No matter what happens."

I nodded with tears in my eyes. "I will do my best, for me and for my boy. No matter what happens, I will not have regrets about this book. I have a good feeling about it. I will publish it somehow. Even if it takes more blood, sweat, and tears, more hard-earned money from my never-ending labour. I will do whatever it takes to publish it – that I do know. And no matter what happens, when I see those words in print, I will be at peace. This is also something that I know. Yes, I will be at peace."

As if she read my mind, Shareena responded, "Yes, Harriet, that is the key. And from whence it came, it will move forward like the tide, like a tidal wave. Once in motion, it will never stop, and yes, you will be the Impetus for what happens next. For it is not just about your boy, but more. Your work will reverberate and resonate throughout all time, affecting and changing the lives of so many people. You do not see, but you will. In time, you will. One action causes another action, and another action. Yes. Yes. Yes. You will See. You Will SEE In Time. I am honoured to meet you. I never thought I would meet you – in this time, in this place. It is truly a gift." She smiled at me and gave me a hug. "Yes, it is an honour. The younglings and the elders would be pleased. You, you are the Start of many things to come. And it's Fortune that I am here with you now."

Suddenly, there was a burst of Light, a ricochet of colour. It was like what it was before, as it was now, but not – all in memories of seasons past, seasons present, seasons in the Future. I took Shareena's hand, and We walked into The Light.

Chapter Six:
Masks

MASKS... Mirrors... I saw the sparkling Light as if it were in my mind's eye. I was walking with Shareena. There was a painting, an art piece, and Shareena told me to close my eyes, which gave me a sense of peace and calm. I opened my eyes, and a golden gazebo appeared. A griffin stepped forward, twinkling gold and magenta.

"Come, my child, come," said the griffin. Shareena nodded at the griffin, and then she disappeared. I walked towards the griffin.

It was like I was in a dream – sleepwalking through time. The sun burst into an orangey-gold orb, and it pulsed like a Heartbeat – a powerful heartbeat. Myriads of colours floated into my mind. Swirls of colour, of Light, and Sound. I entered the Kaleidoscope. Faeries, they were flying around amongst the air tinged with fuchsia. The air – she smelled of roses. I was intoxicated.

The movement, Movement. I came across... There were dragons, wyverns, more griffins, as I had definitely entered another world, beyond the painting. Dream Time, Faerie Time... Then, there was a huge creature, something I had seen before; I thought for a moment. Herodotus, pictures, sketches... It was a Sphinx! But this one was of flesh and bone, and her eyes stared at me, eyes of bright gold and viridian.

"Yes, yes, you are here. It is time to learn. Take this." She handed me a sceptre of gold, rubies, and amethysts. "It is TIME TO – It... IS –" She looked at me intently. "You must learn, you must, and soon."

Suddenly, I saw visions of turrets, a monastery near a lake, a man enrobed in silver, gold, and mauve, and a stained-glass window. I closed my eyes and opened them. Then, there were multitudes of stars. Multitudes. Yes. Yes. Yes. A Multitude. They came. THEY SPOKE. They came. They Heard.

I was on a mountain top, and I heard the howling of The Wind. She was shrieking. SHRIEKING. Yes, the wind was shrieking. She was... A form shaped from this wind, this loud, vocal breath of the Zephyr's daughter. It became a hyenawerewolf, and the sceptre disappeared from my hand, with a dagger appearing instead.

The dagger was made out of dark violet quartz, with a glimmering handle of mother-of-pearl. I looked around. It was just the two of us. I started to rise up into the air... RISE... RISE... RISE.... It STARTED UP – A Dance of Force, A Dance of WILLS. I was remembering these warriors of the past, the Ashanti, and the ones from the Mystical side: the Gods, the Goddesses, the Muses, of which my great-great-grandmother, Tuerini, was one – Mother Mnemosyne's Mystical Line. My arms and legs moved in the air, an aerial ballet.

A beast appeared, a chimera of many colours: amaranthine, gold, silver, and a deep forest green. My blade made contact with the chimera's fangs, then with the beast's long claws. A huge, clanging sound reverberated in the air. I was not deterred – nor was the Beast, then I saw a glimmer – it was a bow and arrow of gold. I reached for it, and it sailed into my hand, with the dagger flying into the sheath on the leather belt around the waist of my silver dress. I took aim and released the arrow, which had a ruby as an arrowhead. It went right into the beast's heart, and I settled back onto the ground.

"You have been victorious. Yes. Two more challenges await you, Harriet," said the sphinx, smiling, while laughing softly, her eyes glowing a deep, bright magenta. I gulped.

Was I up to the task? What was I to learn? What was my purpose? Was it writing, and was there anything else? These questions echoed in my mind.

"Do not take heart," replied the Sphinx, as if she knew what I was thinking. One of the gifts of the Sphinx, in all their ancestral lines, was precognition. The one talking to me, that was her gift, and more, gifts that many others would not have knowledge of, until they actually manifested. "You will be triumphant if you are The One," the Sphinx continued. I nodded but didn't feel too confident.

I entered a room filled with crystal. It shone. There was a peacock of stained glass – she radiated rainbow rays of Light. I gasped.

"Yes, it exists. Yes, you are meant to be here: the world of Dream Land, but also, what is real? What is not? Does it matter? And what will you learn from this? Only you will know. So, Harriet, what do you see?"

I suddenly saw some Adinkra symbols; how I knew what they were, I would never understand, but I did. However, I didn't quite know what each symbol meant or what it represented. I automatically closed my eyes. I felt the synergy, the energy, the frenetic reverie.

"Concentrate. Your mind must flow, and it will reverberate, floating back to you… Yes. Yes." I did so and heard the sound of waves. I visualized the Adinkra symbols from the Ashanti culture. My papa had told me stories about how this language was created to make trade easier with the Romans, but I'm sure there were other reasons for its existence. Papa did tell me, but I couldn't quite remember. I do remember how he would draw some of these symbols in the dirt, behind the cabin where we lived, me, Mama, and Papa.

The Adinkra symbols – they danced in my head. They formed and crashed, along with the waves. I opened my eyes.

"Story," I whispered. "Story."

"Yes…" said the Sphinx and then she disappeared, and in her place was an angel.

The angel was robed in silks: turquoise, scarlet, and emeralds. She smiled.

"You are remembering. You are The Memory, Harriet, and the Messenger Through Story. Don't forget you are a part of a chain –"

Myriads of Light burst forth, crystals of golden Light, magenta too, started to circle in the room, like miniature globes, orbs of colour and magic. "Remember, Harriet," the angel then smiled. "You will get there, with your gifts. Do not despair. Your gifts will bring you many riches, not the ones you are thinking of, but ones that will reverberate Throughout Time, inspiring many generations. Yes, Harriet, Singer Of Song, Lyric Song." The angel with mocha skin and violet hair smiled. Her eyes of emerald sparkled. "You will find your way. Whenever you are in need, call on us; we will always heed your call. Always."

I nodded, my eyes getting glassy. "I understand. I think I have always known."

"Yes, child. Go Forge Your Path. Do not give up now." I nodded again. The angel then disappeared and a dragon – one of amethyst, emerald, and violet wings, but with blood red eyes – greeted me.

"Harriet, we meet. Are you a warrior?" I wasn't sure but knew I would soon find out. A sword fashioned by gnomes and the Aziza appeared in my hand. How did I know that was the sword's origins? Again, I had no answers. How did I know about their creators? Again, the answer eluded me. Seeing this dragon, I immediately started to swerve, moving the sword left and right. The sword made contact with the dragon's paw, and I tried to strike at the dragon, but she was too fast, and I was about to be burnt to a crisp, when another dragon of mauve and gold appeared and breathed out an orb of gold that quickly surrounded me in protection. The dragon spoke – in no uncertain tones – "Leave her. She has nothing left to prove. Leave her be. She has been tested enough."

The other dragon of amethyst, emerald, and violet, nodded in response. She left me alone and disappeared in a puff of smoke.

"Harriet," the mauve and gold dragon called, "come now. You have much to Learn." I nodded, still floating in the orb of gold. It moved in right beside the dragon. "You are curious about your genesis. The Kismet have decided that it is your time, and the Tuatha Dé Danann, the Celts from across the sea, have agreed." I looked surprised, but the dragon was not taken aback. "Yes, it is Time."

She raised a paw – towards the orb holding me, which

drifted toward a toadstool. The orb settled on it. In front of the toadstool was another, and suddenly, it rose up, greeting me with bright, pastel colours of vermilion, sapphire, viridian, and gold. From the toadstool rose up a book: one of pure emerald. She shone in the Light. I opened the book and turned the page. Images, pictures came into my mind of my great-grandmother, coming into the village as a baby, an old man with a long silver beard, who held her in his arms, one woman wrapped in leaves of silver, the other woman in gold, then a couple of sphinxes flashed in front of me, a chair that looked like a throne... I was remembering... Yes, I was remembering... I nodded, then, I was on a plain, a plain with short grass, and trees like a savannah, there were leopards with wings, and then, looking closer, two people holding onto each other, immersed in passion, and a woman saying the name, "Odeione, Odeione, Odeione." And that was when another Story began.

Chapter Seven:
Odeione

GASPS of air. Heat. Their bodies became – She was… Tuerini, daughter of Mother Mnemosyne – she was with the one she loved. It was paradise, looking into his eyes. She didn't know much about him: Soothsayer, poet, he healed people with his passionate words, and now, in his embrace – his touch – she was… An aura of mauve surrounded her, surrounded him; she was swimming in his glow, swimming… Yes. Yes. Yes. She was Swimming. Aura, orbs of Light surrounded them.

Odeione, he was entranced with her – her Light, her Laughter – she was the Only One. The Only. They talked for hours about Story, the importance of oral storytelling, of memories that resurfaced. They talked and talked about these things. He wanted to help his people see the Truth. Some had been so engrossed with Material things, fighting for this and that, like dogs fighting for scraps. When would that end? There was enough food, water, and shelter for everyone. Yet, people were complaining that it wasn't enough… There was a restlessness.

In the time before, there was a struggle, a battle that divided man, woman, and child, but it was over. There was healing, a coming together, and plenty for everyone: live-lihoods realized, whole villages rebuilt. Yet, there was still discontent; Odeione didn't understand. So, he went to the Mountain, Mount Toubkal, for the answer. They say there was a wise man who lived there, enshrouded in mystery and mist, enrobed with silver and gold, with a beard that went on for miles. He sought this man out, travelling for seven days and seven nights. The sun, and then the stars, were his only guides. Yes, he sought to find this wise man, this Soothsayer, who would give him the answer. Yes. Yes. Yes.

He came to the top of the mountain, now enshrouded with ice and snow. He closed his eyes and floated, rising through the air to the very top. To the very top. He saw a door in the side of the wall of ice. He raised his hand, and it opened, for Odeione was of a mystical tribe, connected to The Jinn – connected through Time and Space. For the Svinxians were the hosts of a magical force – a torrent of blue – that would manifest or shape-shift into anything. The Svinxians could be anything they wished, and their lair was in the Sphinx itself, with many tunnels and passage-ways underground. They conducted rituals of magic, filled with incense, myrrh, and other magical elements. They were also connected to the Mystical Ones who went across the sea to the Land Of The Celts, their descendants having jet black hair and swarthy skin.

The Svinxians were also connected to another mys-tical tribe who were possessors of a sword of unmatcha-ble strength, a book that held many secrets, and a harp of crystal and gold – an instrument that sang so sweetly, she would make the hardest, most cynical man cry. They had many more treasures that were kept secret and safe from curious eyes and ears. Yes, they were the Gatekeepers, the Guardians of a land of green punctuated with musical rivers like the River Boyne, whose song also entranced people, making them weep tears of joy. The river goddess, Boann, whose home was near there, was someone he had met on his travels. Yes, his family history was filled with mysticism, mystery, and magic.

Odeione went inside through the doorway. Crystals and chandeliers of ice and snow surrounded him. Mirrors of ice, humming songs of warmth and harmony, reverberated through his mind. He started to get sleepy, but he snapped his fingers, waking himself from the trance, and quickly uttered words of protection from any ominous force that could be waiting. He continued through a passageway, decorated with velvet, rubies, and diamonds. Emeralds also greeted him, singing a sweet, but ominous song. Odeione was on his guard.

A beautiful woman approached him wearing a long dress of ice and snow, the ice sparkling like crystals. "Welcome," she said. "Welcome to Mauretania. You are here to seek him, Adom. He is waiting for you. Come." Odeione followed the tall woman, her red hair aflame with beads of emeralds. He entered another room; it was huge, built like the Colosseum that the Romans had built. The grandeur impressed him.

"Yes, son. This is my lair. Yes. Welcome." Odeione heard a voice but did not know from where. It was musical, not forceful in tone, but with a clear intention and a purpose tinged with patience. He kept walking.

Not far from Odeione was the start of a red carpet — of velvet. A sumptuous crimson carpet. There was a scent, a sumptuous, seductive scent of roses and lotus blossoms – that reached his nose. He felt compelled to sleep but forced his eyes back open.

"Don't fight it, Odeione," the voice said. "Don't. Welcome it."

Odeione continued murmuring a protection chant to himself. He kept walking, down the miles and miles of crimson carpet. Miles and miles. He saw an old man with miles and miles of silvery-grey beard that ran down the crimson velvet carpet. Something told him to look down; as he did, the carpet changed colour – from silver to crimson, then back to silver. He was walking on this man's beard! He thought he had seen everything in life, but No! He was astounded.

"Odeione, approach my chair." Odeione looked; it looked like a throne, but it wasn't. It was a chair made out of beautiful cedar but was decorated with roses, jasmine, and daisies. The chair gave off a seductive scent like the carpet. Odeione approached, and the man looked at him deeply with searing green eyes. "Welcome, Odeione. Welcome. You are here for answers as you have questions. Come. Speak. Ask your questions."

Odeione did, one of them being, "Why are my people so unhappy with so much plenty?"

The wise man asked, "What do they do during the time of the rising sun?"

Odeione replied that at first, when it was necessary, people had to work, have livelihoods, to survive; but then riches came manyfold, so that was no longer necessary. The people often lazed about, bathing in the sun, sometimes talking, sometimes in silence.

"What is missing, Odeione?"

"What is missing?" asked Odeione out loud, puzzled

by the question.

Odeione thought for a moment. "Purpose," he answered. "Purpose. People need a purpose, a reason to rise to the morning sun."

The man nodded. "You know what you have to do. Stay awhile. Sleep. You can stay in the guest quarters. The journey back for you will be long." Odeione nodded.

Two women wrapped in leaves of gold and silver accompanied him to his guest chambers. Odeione slept for what seemed like days but was actually not even hours. When he woke, a silver plate of grapes and cheese awaited him. He ate hungrily, gulping the food down. He looked under the blankets. He was wearing sleepwear of the finest silk and magenta. How did that happen? How? He saw his travelling clothes on a chair and got dressed. He left the chambers and went into the hallway. It was quiet – too quiet. He listened. He waited. He listened. He walked further down the passageway. No sign of anyone, not even those women wrapped in leaves of gold and silver. He entered the chamber, the chamber where the wise man sat, and gave counsel. He walked up the long trail of crimson carpet. It didn't change colour. He walked up closer to the old man; he looked like he was sleeping, but Odeione had a feeling that he wasn't. The old man's head was down. He touched his head gently. The old man's eyes opened, but they looked pale, like opaque glass.

"Go," he cried, "Go!" Odeione looked behind him quickly – it was a chimera – with blood flowing from his veins, dark green blood.

"Step aside!" the chimera shouted. "Step ASIDE!" Odeione wouldn't, feeling compelled to protect the old man. "No?" The chimera then laughed. "Very well," he said, and breathed a cloud of burning fire. Odeione closed his eyes, and a shield appeared, protecting him and the old man. "Step back, or you will pay the price!" the chimera warned. "Youngling, you have no right to challenge me! Step aside!"

"No," replied Odeione.

"Then, feel my wrath." The chimera closed his eyes and breathed deeply. When he opened them, a wall of fire surrounded the room. Odeione gulped, but he would not back down. He would not be deterred. He closed his eyes and took a deep breath. He then exhaled slowly. A wall of water, a flood, an ocean gushed toward the chimera. The wall of fire disappeared, and the force of water was so strong, it knocked the chimera against a wall of ice that suddenly appeared. The chimera was dead.

"Quick. Go to your village." The old man said the words in determined, staccato tones. "The other chimeras know what you have done. They are psychically connected. Hurry, save your people. I will give you Chione, Sister of the Sphinx in Egypt. She is the guardian of this realm. Hurry, my son. Thank you for saving my life. I am indebted to you. I will always be of service to you, always. Now. Hurry."

The sphinx of gold and silver, smelling of myrrh and incense, flew toward Odeione. She touched down, bowing her head. Odeione climbed on, and the Sphinx nodded at the old man. In a flash, Odeione was in the air on the mystical, magical creature. Chione said, "Try not to be concerned. I'll get there as soon as I can. Have faith." Before you know it, Odeione was back at the village.

It was already in flames, riddled with chimeras blowing flames of fire at villagers, their huts, and all that they held dear. Terror flooded the air. Screams pierced Odeione's eardrums. He flew into action. He raised his arms toward the sky, and many people appeared – some looking like him, some not, men, women, for the Svinxians had the gift of not only shape-shifting but putting their consciousness into other beings from their Imagination. DreamMaking was Queen.

This Army Of Imagination started battling the chimeras, cutting off heads, kicking, using swords, the martial arts of jujitsu, taught to them by monks, druids from the Isle of green, armed this magical force.

The villagers saw what was happening and also jumped into action. The force of The Mystical and the force of The Mortal united against Evil. The villagers and the mystical force got the upper hand. The army of chimeras was destroyed. The village was safe. The village had found its purpose.

The old man looked at a mirror, a mystical one made out of the ice from Mount Kilimanjaro. It was a land, not just of desert, but also ice and snow. A land of contradictions. Adom nodded and then smiled. "Yes," he said simply.

The village had found its purpose, awakening something inside that had been asleep for years. The village decided to always have some projects to revitalize the community, and to go forward to help others in need, for they understood that everyone needed a purpose – even in a time of plenty – or else vices like greed and jealousy would fester like a disease. Odeione was happy.

What had happened with the Army Of Chimeras was not a good thing, but at least his village had woken up and found itself – for even in a time of plenty, one can lose one's direction. Odeione had told his love, Tuerini, this. She agreed. But on one of his journeys to another village, to help others, it was found out that one chimera from that Army was still alive and wanted vengeance against Odeione for the death of his brother, even though it was in self-defence. This chimera, Kerukoo, didn't care. He wanted blood. Odeione's blood. He would not be denied. Odeione told Tuerini this as she was now with child. She understood, agreeing with what Odeione had done in self-defence while the village was at war with the Army Of Chimeras. She even agreed and believed what Odeione did was right, saving the old man. But Odeione then remembered what the old man said and asked for his help. The man heard him telepathically and answered, "Whenever you seek my help, I will give it." Odeione heard him and nodded, telling Adom what had happened. The baby was born in secret, and the two held the baby close.

The old man appeared with the two tall women enrobed with leaves of gold and silver, their skin sparkling a deep, dark, cerulean. The man said, "I will take the child and give her protection. Any other children will also be protected. Prayers are not always answered in the way you expect, but remember, everything happens for a reason." The two nodded. The baby, smiling, but somehow sadness touching those lips, while knowing the old man wouldn't bring her any harm. The old man nodded at the couple and stood holding the child. The women, one on each side, stood beside him, and the four disappeared in smoke. Tuerini cried but knew it was for the best. Odeione, now her husband as they had also married in secret, also shed a few tears. It was indeed for the best.

The couple had two more children, but both died in

childbirth. The couple then decided it was best to just focus on each other and travel to different worlds, helping many realms to find their purpose through Story and Song. Tuerini was the goddess of Poetry, Justice, and Healing, the tenth daughter of Mother Mnemosyne, and Odeione was the god of Poetry to his people. They loved. They laughed. They loved until the End Of Time, as they had decided to remain human to be of even more service to other Mortal Ones. When the time had come for them to cross over, they did, entering the Gates of Pubinim, where they would reign forever.

The child? The old man took her to a village in the Ashanti empire, where she was adopted by a tribe the old man could trust. She grew up intelligent, beautiful, and most importantly, compassionate. The young woman, Dhakirah, then got married and had children of her own, including one daughter. She was also gifted with song, the song of words and story.

She was ten, playing in her village with a doll when they came, men with pale skin and chains. This young girl was placed on a ship – a ship filled with Death, headed for a land that would have an ominous future for her and her people. People with a rich history, with mocha or cocoa skin, who were not seen as human beings but as human cargo, free labour for a system riddled with greed. A world of darkness and sadness, a world, a country, a nation among many that would need hope. A child who came across that shore, and that girl, was Boahinmaa.

***

Boahinmaa, she was my grandmother, and I, Harriet E. Wilson, was her granddaughter, and inherited her penchant for Story, For Lyrical Song. I would go on to be an author. Me, Harriet, a poet, but I also think an author of other genres, especially what I was working on next. I was the next lover of song, lyric song, manifesting into different forms, and being the great-great-great-granddaughter of the Goddess Of Memory, Mother Mnemosyne, and a reflection of my grandmother, Boahinmaa. The name echoed in the chambers of my mind. My grandmother. The child of the Mystical One, Dhakirah. And Dhakirah was the daughter of Tuerini, one of the twin daughters of Mother Mnemosyne. I smiled. Yes, Mother Mnemosyne was my great-great-great-grandmother. Me, Harriet, I was learning all about my Story, and it filled me with Joy. I was on my way, and it was just The Beginning.

Chapter Eight:
Cara

I'M trying to Hold On... Me, Cara, three miscarriages, no child to call my own. Yes, it wasn't the right time, I could have been a teenage mother, and now I am nineteen... I'm just trying to find my way. They say: female, Mother, the "natural," as prescribed role, yes, we can work, but still it's expected... to be a Mother, be a Mother. I'm trying to hold on – another job not going well – I'm trying to find the "silver lining," but it's choking me with its silk cord, choking me...

My mother said, "Hold on, Hold On, better times are coming." But when? I'm trying so hard, where are the opportunities? My mom said, "I felt like you did, it will get better." Better? But when? I've been in the same place for years, so, when, mama, when will things change?

Then, I see a woman in emerald, wearing garlands, three-tiered like a wedding cake. She appears in my dreams. I told my mother, and at first, she said nothing. Then one day, she told me about an adventure she had: she saw a stag, then it became a woman, all aglow, like a kaleidoscope, with shards of Light emanating from her body. She took her to other worlds, and she met a child, one who would save all worlds. Then, two women, tall ones – one with eyes of piercing blue, took her back. I felt like it had never happened, but then my mom took something out of a small cedar chest that she had. She opened it up, and there it was – a pocket watch – gleaming different colours. She gave it to me.

"The tall woman said whenever I felt despair, to take this out, open it, and look at the face of the watch. It took me to different worlds, sometimes for years at a time, though it was only a day in ours. It helped me. It will help you. The doors will open. I know you want to be a visual artist, to do your art, make a part-time living, and then one day, a full-time one. I see how hard you work at your job to make ends meet. I see how you are trying, and it breaks my heart. I know nothing, I don't have any connections in that world, the arts, and in terms of getting a better job to support yourself, I can't help you. Your uncle would have, my brother, but he died years ago. Heart failure. Taking care of everyone else except for himself. We have to take care of ourselves first; if not, we have nothing to give others. I give this to you, the only thing I can give you. I hope it helps. I do love you, Cara. I do. I wish I could do more. I wish I could. That's all I have, and this..." She placed something else gently in my hands. It was a journal of a deep cyan, with golden gilded pages that shone in the light. "They said it was hers, the Chosen One, and had poetry in it like the one that was published in a newspaper."

I wondered who wrote this poetry? Who was the author? My mom just smiled as if she knew what I was thinking and said, "When you read it, you will know." I shrugged, not sure what she meant, but went along with it. So many things these days just did not make sense to me.

My mom left the room, and I looked at the book. It was a striking cyan, with gilded edges, and a beautiful scent emanated from it, making me feel at ease right away. Yes, it was the key, but how?

I decided to go for a walk. It was a dull winter day, no sun, just grey. Just grey. It was just so desolate, so desolate, and the landscape cried out for sun and rain so the green, emerald carpet could return. I felt like crying out, screaming out for that too. I felt something. I walked to an area of black wrought iron fences, some with lions forged onto the black laced gates of metal and orbs of Light shining through the snow, as if forcing their way through the darkness. There was a clearing. Birch trees. Evergreens. There was a Stillness. A calm. So eerie. I waited and waited. Hoped for something, but not sure what.

I saw a stag. Instinctively, I showed the pocket watch, and then the cyan journal gilded with gold pages. The stag nodded. Then, a woman appeared where the stag stood. She motioned for me to come closer. I did. I walked even closer, and then she flew over to me, wings came out from nowhere, wings with flowers, bluebells, daisies, and carnations. "She gave them to you. It was meant to be. Come. It is time. You must find your way."

I took her hand, and we both rose into the air. A hole opened up, and swirls of colour started to turn, rotate, then spin quickly – bursts of aquamarine, gold, viridian, and amaranth. "Don't be afraid – it's the Doorway." I nodded. I followed her, floating in the air, like a puppet, and surged forward. We both entered. It was dark, then bursts of Light – Stars – lots of them. Stars. I smiled. It had been a long time since I felt any joy. A long time. I had to keep going, but I felt like I was slipping over the edge, and I was about to plummet to my Death. "It is not your time yet, Young One. Youngling, it isn't. Just keep going. But right now, don't think about that. Just close your eyes. Just close your eyes. Just. You have to Just..." I did, and there it was... oceans, waves of peace, calm, and hope.

"We are here," she said. "We are here." I later found out her name was Sigatta, and she had taken my mother many years ago to this Mystical place where I knew that anything was possible.

***

"She looks like her mother," said a tall woman with piercing blue eyes.

"Yes," said another with blue hair and violet eyes. "Yes, funny how that works. It was meant to be."

"Yes," said the other woman. "Indeed."

I stood aghast. These were the two women Mom had talked about. I later found out the one with rose-coloured hair and the unforgettable blue eyes was Oceantis, and the younger woman with bright blue hair and violet eyes was Staerkie, her cousin.

"Yes, Youngling," said the purple-eyed one, "we are the ones your mother mentioned. It was not her time; it was not her destiny. It's yours." It was as if this younger woman had read my mind. The purple-eyed woman smiled at me, knowing exactly what I was thinking, and had a chuckle at my realization.

"What destiny? I don't understand," I said soon after.

"You are the Vargentian. You are the Pocantian. But more importantly, you are the Key to unite all worlds – by saving Her."

"Who?" I whispered.

"The one they speak of." I still looked confused, so the woman continued, "The One With Words That Will Change Time. The one who will not only give hope, but send a wave of change, for all, not only for those persecuted, but for those in any way connected to the evil.

I must have still looked confused, so the woman smiled and said, "The great-great-great-granddaughter of the Mystical One, Mother Mnemosyne — her twin daughter, Tuerini, who had many gifts besides the gift of poetry, loved an Egyptian, as did her mother. Tuerini gave birth to a daughter who had to go into hiding, and that daughter gave birth to a baby girl who would later become the grandmother of the one who is The Messenger, the one who will save all worlds." An inkling started to swim around in my brain. Rivers of Memory — a book... Cyan with gilded gold pages, that my mom gave me...

"Harriet," I whispered.

"Yes, Harriet." The woman with violet eyes nodded. "We will have to travel through different worlds, swim in oceans of stars, and enter black holes to find her, and it will not be easy. You, you are your Mother's Daughter. She told you about The Child?"

I nodded. "Well," the woman continued, "Harriet's great-grandmother, the Child, came into our care, and then, she had to be hidden. Your mother, Kerianna, thought she would be the Guardian, the Warden, the Warrior to protect Her. That was not her role. That was not her Path. You are the Guardian and the Warrior who will protect The Messenger, who is the great-granddaughter of that baby girl, the one we had to protect. Harriet will be in your care. We all have different paths, different gifts to bestow, to make the world a better place. You will find out what else you are meant to do, in Time."

I looked at her, amazed. Me, the Guardian? A Warrior? The two women smiled at me.

"There is more to come," said the taller one with magenta-coloured hair and the striking blue eyes. "There is more to come. You will see." The shorter woman, with hair of a shining teal and bright violet eyes, nodded. I thought to myself, I think they were right. There is more To Come.

"Then, it will begin," said the taller woman with rose coloured hair and blue eyes. "The Journey within a Journey, traversing Time And Space. Let us begin."

The woman started to hum, and then it was Darkness. Then, it was Light. It was murky at first, the air, but then I saw – a sword, a mirror, and a book. They were spinning like they were in their own orbit. Other books were doing the same. The woman with violet eyes just motioned for it, and it answered her Call. She looked at it. She closed her eyes, opened up her arms, and then it was Darkness again. Then Light. I saw fire. I heard screams. I saw creatures I had never seen before: ninki nankas, as Oceantis explained to me later, as well as flying Sphinxes, like the one from Egypt, and blood – so much blood. We got closer. The woman with flowing rose-coloured hair held the hand of the woman with teal hair and violet eyes.

Suddenly, we were on the battlefield. A sword appeared in my hand. "I don't know what to do," I screamed over the loud din of clashing metal.

"You will," said Staerkie, the woman with violet eyes, now turning emerald. "They will come back. The memories, they come back." A creature came at me with fangs, large bespeckled eyes, and skin the colour of dark sand. The woman nodded. "Yes, they will come back."

I suddenly started doing backflips, then, using my sword, throwing daggers that appeared out of nowhere. "Yes, it has just Begun," said Staerkie, smiling. "Yes, it has Just Begun."

The two women started to hum in unison, and multiple reflections of themselves came forward. For the two women were from a mystical tribe that came across the seas to a land of Green and Mist. They went underground, as the ones from Ships crashed their shores. In time, there were others of a more swarthy complexion, who became part of an ancestral line descended from those who came from the land of desert and pyramids. From the land of the guardian, The Sphinx, who had many sisters, brothers, and also came from a long ancestral line. That is what they told me. The stories I have in my mind, instilled with rivets of Memory.

I was doing an operatic ballet – jujitsu, karate, all the Martial arts – killing creatures left and right. When we were done, there were bodies everywhere. The two women talked to others who looked just like them. And then, we disappeared, reappearing on a rugged mountain top.

72

Chapter Nine:
The Land Of Mist

THE tall woman with flaming rose-coloured hair, Oceantis, thought for a moment. Reams of symbols were running through her mind... The language of the Druids, and the Akan...the Adinkra language. She then looked down at Staerkie with a meditative look in her eyes, as if she was being told something. I was with the two women and wondered what was next?

"The ones from across the sea told me where to find The Messenger – especially the One, Protector Of All Poets, Storytellers, and Bards, Brigid. She told me just now where to find The Spark – for All Of Us. She is under the care of The Snow Queene."

"Eberveen?"

"Yes, Eberveen. She knows her importance, the one with the gift of song, lyrical song. She is protecting her and knows who and what she is."

"How will we find her?"

"The Book." A tome of ruby red appeared in her hands. "But first, we must go forth to a place, a sphere of natural beauty and calm. We must go to Gougane Barra."

"The sanctuary of Saint Fin Barre?"

"Yes, the Ancient ones deemed it so, and from there to see this One, The Poet, The Storyteller, that Eberveen is sheltering. From there, it continues; from there, it ends. But from this is also The Beginning. Yes, Sister, to Gougane Barra."

The other woman agreed. "Yes," she said, while she nodded. The two Sisters and I disappeared and reappeared on an ocean of clouds, way up in the sky. It was like we were on top of the world. We were sitting on clouds, and the clouds of gold and orange floated, but really, they flew – like birds to the chapel, the famed chapel surrounded by the Shehy mountains. With this restful journey on the clouds, I had read the journal, the cyan journal with golden gilded pages. The first poem to reach my eyes was "Fading Away," and then I read the rest. Somehow, I knew that one was published, and later I would find out that my hunch was right. "Fading Away" was published in The Farmer's Cabinet. And that poem, I believed, showed me that I was not alone, and that the obstacles that I was facing in trying to do anything, let alone being an artist, were challenging. I suddenly noticed how the sunset was appearing like a golden tone on my mocha skin and took a moment to feel the warmth of the setting sun. I had hoped to meet the poetess of this work in this lifetime. Staerkie and Oceantis told me that they were going to meet the Messenger. I knew that the Time was close. The Time Was Close. And then, we all descended, the clouds descended, becoming mist, and our feet touched the emerald ground that was Gougane Barra. We were at a monastery that, at some times of the year, was almost entirely surrounded by water. We went to the area where people went to pray. There were different stations, different areas where people would pray, in succession, for people in pain, suffering in other ways, or battling some kind of illness. Then, we saw a range of beautiful mountains framed by golden sunlight. We then held hands and saw rays of Light shooting forth into the sky. Then, we saw him. Saint Fin Barre. The founder of Gougane Barra and Corcaigh. He was dressed in robes of white, garnet, and ultramarine. His eyes of deep, dark brown glistened.

"Yes, Sisters," he spoke. "I knew you would come. You are here to see the Snow Queene."

"Yes," said Oceantis, "and to –"

"Yes, follow me," said Saint Fin Barre, who seemed in a hurry. I had a feeling that time was fleeting, and there was a sense of urgency. Oceantis was thinking the same thing, as there was a serious gleam in her bright blue eyes. Saint Fin Barre took us inside the monastery, where there was a stained-glass window with his likeness.

"Step inside," he said, gesturing with one hand. We stepped into the painting of glass, and then there was a door – a flaming shade of red – a half circle of oak. We opened it, and there was a wonderland of ice and snow, a palace gleaming white and cobalt. Saint Fin Barre nodded. He then disappeared. The Snow Queene, a petite woman wearing high-heeled boots and a cape of fuchsia, she smiled.

"Welcome, Sisters." She smiled again. "Welcome. You are here to see her, The One who will unite all our worlds, including her own. Come," she gestured with one hand. "Come." We walked into a chamber of velvet walls and rugs of white fur, and bookcases of willow that surrounded us like a circle. The ceiling was decorated with chandeliers of the finest ice crystals that glittered a bright mauve, gold, and emerald. They seemed to sing as the crystals moved, like they were dancing in the air. I was entranced. Then, I looked around, and there she was: a woman with the warmest brown eyes, in a coat trimmed with white fur, and a matching cap of crimson. The author. The author of the poems in that beautiful journal was before me: it was Harriet E. Wilson. We were meant to meet.

The woman looked at me, and I met her gaze. I then just ran into her open arms. We embraced, and I cried. I felt that I was home, at last. The woman with teal hair, Staerkie, just beamed, and so did Oceantis, who was actually her cousin. But the two women were so close, they saw each other as Sisters.

Later, Staerkie said to Harriet, "You are a part of us, and Tuerini – she is in you. You are home, now." Harriet smiled and hugged her back. There were other women, faeries, women from Tuatha Dé Danann, and other mystical wise women who knew of books, stories from the Ages. They knew all the Masters like Homer, Pope, Shakespeare, and so on. They probably had met Homer. But with their knowledge of the Classic Arts from her world, they also had a culture of their own. The Snow Queene mentioned the Tuatha Dé Danann, those who came from across the seas to the land of Emerald. The Queen also mentioned the ones who came from Egypt, and how some of the people from the mystical land of mist and green were descendants from the land of desert and the Nile, some having dark, swarthy features.

The Snow Queene also mentioned her own Sisters from the Akan empire, and how she met some of those ancestors. She had also been to the Mountain of Ice And Snow, part of the lands also known for the Desert, the pyramids, and the realm of The Sphinx. The Snow Queene then explained Harriet's genesis, how she was the great-great-great-granddaughter of Mother Mnemosyne.

I saw in Harriet's eyes that she couldn't believe it, that she would meet all these powerful women: some were goddesses, such as of the moon, and so on. I couldn't believe, not in this lifetime, that I would have such an experience. These women, many Sisters, watched over Harriet, and I think me as well, when we felt the most despair. They helped us to survive. Now, it all made sense.

I also met Selena, who also came from the land North of the 49th parallel. She was a companion to Anisie, and Selena was also becoming a warrior. I then met Stargette, the unforgettable Cosmic Orb Of Light and Sound, who had her own language, and her people spanned many Millennia, even before Time herself. I knew now that I was on the right Path. Something would change in me, and I knew that I would find my way here, with these women. I think my mom would have been happy for me. I just hope that I can see her again and tell her what I have seen, and what I have learnt, that she is a part of this too.

Yes, the Music was in Harriet. I saw that – me, Cara – and because of that, I saw that Harriet had a passion for poetry, and lyrical song. The Snow Queene told Harriet about how her great-grandmother was the daughter of Tuerini, the twin sister to the Muse for Poetry, and how Tuerini's birth came about: it was a love affair Mother Mnemosyne had with an Egyptian soothsayer. And wasn't it ironic that her daughter, Tuerini, would also fall in love with an Egyptian herself? Yes, paths crossed, paths forged, paths that repeat again. Yes, such is Life – such is Love. Harriet understood better.

Harriet's great-grandmother always seemed different to the other women. She dreamed a lot. Read a lot too. Learnt languages, especially Arabic, quickly; she also seemed to know things before they happened. Her daughter was the same way, which would have been Harriet's grandmother. The other villagers noticed, too, but didn't say anything. They were both accepted members of that tribe and were loved. Harriet sensed that and felt that love herself. Yes, she felt that love herself in this wonderland forged in ice and snow. Yes, it all made sense. And yes, there was more to come. As Harriet talked to the other two women, Oceantis and Staerkie, part of The Kismet, I knew something was amiss – something was rising, something that wasn't good, and that I, as well as Harriet, would be a part of that battle to put things right.

I think Harriet knew, like I did, that everyone had their role, their part to play – everyone had their path, and one of the purposes of this Life was to figure out what it was, and to make this world, all worlds, a better place.

Chapter Ten:
Kerianna: The One Who Went Before

ME, Kerianna, I inherited this name from my grandmother, and I am already heralding a Herstory, carving out Stories Through Time. Me Listening, Listening – Memory, Memory, Mystery – what is my purpose? What is my voice? I am Remembering, And My Daughter, Cara? I asked, "What was My Purpose?" The Kismet, They were my family, and then I was sent back – I'm trying to understand. My daughter, Cara, now she has gone; it's only been six hours, but will she be all right? I gave her the book of cyan, the gleaming gold pocket watch; I told her that those things were the key. They Were The Key. Was I wrong to send her on that Journey?

What will she find? I don't know. I hope that she is safe, going to the place where I saw the stag.

Nothing.   I   have   heard   Nothing.

I have to wait, you see, I just have to wait. Until then, I will continue to light a candle, to light A Candle, and take a moment; close my eyes, I have to take a moment, and until she comes back,

I   Have   To   Dream.

***

Seventus: the Crescent moon, arising in shards of light. She appeared before me – Sigatta – she was snow glistening like diamonds, the lights shining like sunken golden orbs in the snow. Radiations Of Light appeared. She smiled. I need relief – no, direction. I approached. She turned into a stag, then a snowshoe hare, then a gladiator with a Roman helmet shining gold, with red plumage on top, a feather – she beckoned to me, and I followed, riding ribbons of air and light, as I ascended. She nodded, and before I knew it, I was flying, looking at the sunset, a sunken sliver of burning orange. The Terwillegar Bridge was before me, her Sister not far away, ribbons of blue on the ice, ribbons of blue, purple, orange burnt into the sky. I laughed, for the first time in months. I felt free, I raised my arms, like an albatross, flying for the first time. She smiled at me, violet eyes glistening. I closed my eyes instinctively – when I opened them, I saw bursts of stars, comets, and The Milky Way – a kaleidoscope of colour and sound, for stars emit a heartbeat, a pulsating crescendo of sound, that reverberates through the galaxies. I saw Beings of Light with long dresses of azure, violet, and gold, and they jumped on these beams of Light and rode them like motorcycles, racing across the universe – I was entranced. The woman with purple eyes looked at me and took my hand.

Me, Kerianna, I suddenly felt a sense of peace. I then noticed a door – gleaming green – she, Sigatta, nodded again. I opened it, and my life was never the same. Would it be the same for my daughter, Cara? I sense her presence, even though she is not with me. She is somewhere else, but I sense a rising joy in her. It makes me smile, but I hope she is safe, even though I know she is at peace.

More memories are flying back to me, and I see more – I understand my roles and what I am supposed to be... Not just as Mother, but when my time would be coming. But for now, I am on a different path, and I will just accept how my course is being charted – a different course, a different path – that is what I have to see. And I do. The currents of memory continue to wash on my shore. I will continue to propel forward, and I hope my girl – my Cara – is all right. She is following another path that Sigatta, the Faerie of Many Lights, took her on – where she is, I don't know, but I know that is where she needs to be. But for now, I must remember what my role is and what is to be. I have no crystal ball, so I close my eyes and Remember.

Two women flew to a mountain top – a craggy one – topped with an icy crevasse just at the tip, the precipice. They said, "We must find the One who will unite all worlds; the One who is The Messenger Of Hope." The women, one with rose-coloured hair and piercing blue eyes, the other with unforgettable teal hair and violet eyes, jumped off the mountain top and grew wings, flying through the air like arrows. They landed in a land of mirrors. I saw all this and was amazed. How did they do that?

Once they landed, they saw me, a young woman oddly dressed. Who was this creature? They noticed that the top part of my body and my legs were covered with what they thought was a strange blue material. I, Kerianna, dressed in denim, was about to speak when a faerie, gleaming with light, appeared.

The faerie spoke. "It's me, Oceantis and Staerkie – it's Sigatta." The tall young faerie glittered like millions of shards of glass. She twinkled as she talked. "She is with me," she said, pointing to what I'm sure they thought was an oddly dressed girl. "It is all right. Her name is Kerianna." I couldn't believe my eyes.

I flew through time and space, space and time, through an ocean of burning persimmon, a glowing fire, following this mystical woman who first appeared as a stag. I walked on a path punctuated with a black wrought iron fence that had fleur-de-lis glittering like golden tips of light in the early evening. I couldn't believe how fresh the air felt that evening. The snow was crisp, and my feet were crunching through the white powder. I had my winter boots on and was wearing my coat with a wool scarf around my neck. But then I saw a magenta orb in the distance and, as I walked closer, I noticed it was a stag. She motioned to me and changed into a faerie. I followed her, taking her out-stretched hand without a thought, and we started flying through the air, rising higher up into the stratosphere; I had never felt so free. Now, up here, I knew that my life would never be the same, and in that same moment, I had an inkling that there would be another who would also have a chance to change – to transform, to delve into a meta-morphosis.

I realized I had tuned out for a moment and had to focus again on what the three women were saying.

"She is with me," continued Sigatta. "We are here to find her – the babe, the key to everything. She is some-where in these woods. Help us. Without her, our worlds will never be the same."

The Sisters nodded. They waded through swamps, crossed rivers, and flew across canyons, but there was no sign of this babe. Then, a piercing scream rang out. All the women stopped. One got ready her bow and arrow and took aim. The arrowhead gleamed blood red and left the bow – it sailed through the air and found its mark. There was silence, followed by a Thump. Then something came floating through the air, away in the distance and coming closer. It was a Baby in swaddling clothes. They were damp and dirty. The Sister with the bow twisted her wrist slightly, and the clothes turned into reams of clean cotton and silk of a bright rose. The baby floated into her arms. She was safe. The baby had shining eyes of green with the most gorgeous skin of cocoa. She had wisps of jet black, curly hair framing her face. She looked at the woman, the tall woman with eyes of icy blue... and bright pink hair that tumbled down her shoulders. The woman spoke, "Yes, Child. You are here with us, and safe."

I came forward, outfitted in my jeans and a denim top, and held out my hands. "Can I hold her?" The woman with eyes of icy blue nodded and handed me the Baby. It felt good to hold the baby. I felt, somehow, that this little one represented so much Possibility, of doorways that could be opened, endless doorways – that, somehow, it would rub off on me, and I would also start anew. Staerkie, the young woman with shocking blue hair and violet eyes, sensed my emptiness and gently touched my shoulder. I smiled back gingerly and continued to hold this beautiful miracle.

I had no direction. I worked in retail at an upscale boutique store in an area that echoed the unique niche stores found in Europe. I was trying to get into a management position, but people less qualified than me were getting these positions instead, and I didn't know what to do. I had a business degree after graduating from an accelerated two-year degree program, but I just wasn't getting there. I just felt like giving up, because despite having the necessary skills and background, I still wasn't getting the chances. It was just so frustrating. Sigatta sensed what I was feeling and squeezed my hand. I was constantly surprised by what these women knew without me saying a word.

The woman with eyes of piercing blue and bright pink hair, Oceantis, approached the tall woman emanating rays of light, my guide on this journey. They exchanged a few words, then both women chanted words that I didn't recognize. Then they said, "Yes, that is where it will begin."

Over time, I grew in confidence with the support of the Sisters from The Kismet and read many of their books that talked about the Power Of Story, the importance of finding your own path, and the belief that your destiny will be revealed. They all talked about song, the lyrical music, poetry, and the soothsayers, the poets. I even trained with a sword and learnt the martial arts of defense, jujitsu, and so on. The woman smiled. "Soon, you'll be Ready." They smiled. And the child – she grew by leaps and bounds every day, but eventually she had to return to the tribe. The women had created a new, stronger spell to protect her from any would-be captors. With this new spell, the tribe who were raising her would be better protected. The women, this Sisterhood, were always able to find a solution, which inspired me to do the same – especially in terms of my own life.

Then one night, the moon descended – a silver slice, a glimmering silver crescent in the dark sky of black velvet. I was dreaming of A Book, A Sword, A Flame, and A Quill. "What does it all mean?" I thought, immersed in the river of dreams. As I slept, waves of water appeared before me, and then a young black woman with hair swept up into a bun wearing a simple but vibrant aquamarine dress appeared. She had a quill in her hand and was sat at a desk.

The young woman was deep in thought and surrounded by the glow of a lantern. I started to murmur in my sleep. When I woke up, I was standing at a gate – a black wrought iron gate – with sunken golden orbs of Light shining from below the snow. The trees were dark black silhouettes etched against the cerulean sky, a sky of deep dark aquamarine. There was silence.

"What am I to be ready for?" I thought. "Wasn't I meant to stay with The Kismet? I thought that was my place." Tears came to my eyes. Then I saw it – rather her – the stag surrounded by a magenta, viridian, and sapphire halo. She glowed. The animal nodded, then disappeared. That is what I saw when I first met the Woman of Light, Sigatta. I walked home. When I got there, peering at the clock, I realized that I had only been gone for three hours, but it felt like three years with The Kismet. I could neither believe it nor understand what had just happened. One of the Sisters appeared outside my apartment. Another appeared beside her.

"She thought she was meant to stay with us."

"I know," the one with stark blue eyes replied. "But that is not her path. No, there are other things she must do. She must live this life as a mortal first. It is not time yet for her to be at the next level, to reach the Land Of Oeurs. No, it is not time yet."

"She is one of those – She is a Messenger, Embodying Memory, and a Warrior..."

"Yes, Staerkie," the woman with the burgundy rose hair replied. "That is what she is, but it is not time yet. She must remain among the Mortal Ones for now. Then, when it is Time, the next journey will begin."

"How do you know, Oceantis?" replied the Sister with

fiery blue hair and purple eyes.

"I don't – I just follow the signs of the Ones from Before – the Tuatha Dé Danann, who came from across the sea. They have told me of what is to pass. And now, to find the other, who is The Key." The tall woman with piercing blue eyes heard the sound of loud thunder. She looked down at the young woman with bright purple eyes and blue hair.

Chapter Eleven:
M

MOTHER Mnemosyne, wield your magic... your sceptre of velvet and ice, your sceptre of rubies and gold. Touch my hand and take me into the Other World... take me to the Land Of Faerie... I, Harriet, am residing in the castle forged from ice and snow, the lair of Queen Eberveen, but I know that soon I will be on another Journey. I am thinking... Swimming through Waking dreams... My eyes, still Wide Open – the Land Of Faerie, I want to sail on rivers of thoughts, go on ships of memory, and ride on the billowing sails of creativity before they pause on islands of imagination forged by the mind Sparks Of Light, Sparks Of Energy.

Mother Mnemosyne, take me away to different worlds where there is no pain, no regret, no doubt, just joy – dancing with elves, dwarves, and giants. Take me away to another time, another place, where my countenance, the colour of my skin, doesn't make a difference. Mother Mnemosyne, take me away to a world filled with Possibility, where I can truly fly with wings of Hope... Where obstacles are only in the Mind. Mother, Mother Mnemosyne – I am lost when I am not with you, for you remind me of the Ancestors from the Ashanti line...

I think of my mother with the bright almond brown eyes – my Irish mother from the line of the Celts – and I think of all things, Mother Mnemosyne – streams and rivers of Recollection, of Days gone by when The Word was the spark, when monarchs and the Arts soared, patrons were gateways, storytellers were respected as lyric soothsayers. Oh, Mother Mnemosyne, how much longer must I linger in this place, linger in the landscape of obstacles... This Boston... I look down at the glowing light mahogany tone of my skin. I am selling hair products to restore colour from grey, going door to door – it is not easy, and rejection is so much of a reality. Oh, Mother Mnemosyne, you remind me of the gods, the ancestors of old that my mother told me of, like Brigid, the mystical one who Emanates Story, and the Tuatha Dé Danann, who I know I will meet soon. You also remind me of my African ancestors. My father told me of those who came across the ocean in chains from the Akan empire – scholars, philosophers, architects, astronomers... He told me not to forget, that we had a glorious history, a history that they wanted to destroy by murdering our Memories... Yes, Papa, I remember that too. He told me how his mother talked about the elders sitting around the fire, and the only sound was the comforting presence of Silence, the sky dotted with golden orbs of light, and the shooting stars, silver and light saffron streaks reaming and streaming into infinity. I remember what Papa told me. And now this place, this Boston – how can I hold on? Boston... But I try. I try and try and try. My gift – this pen, this quill, how will it free my son, and can we create a new Life together, a place where we can both blossom and grow roots? Is that possible?

Mother Mnemosyne, I get tired. There are those whom I have not met yet – Brigid, the Akan, echoing the triumphs of Egypt, and the Tuatha Dé Danann – yet, through my mother's stories, I feel like I know you all. But I am so tired. Where do I go from here? A book is coming, a torrent of words, images, about my life, but also a homage to my ancestors from across the seas, an ode to how we all Survive, somehow. You are the Bridge, all of you, The Mystical Ones – to understanding, getting The Word out, and then, hopefully, saving my son from the prison that is poverty.

And Mama, Papa, I cry so many nights. So many nights I feel alone, and so what do I do? I cling onto bits. I cling onto stardust, trickles of times I had with you, Papa, and Mama; before you, Papa, walked into the Other World, a place inhabited by the Celestial Ones, a place amongst the stars. Papa, I wish I was there with you. I love you, too, Mama, but you are also gone, having entered the celestial gates. In my mind's eye, I know you are there and are now at eternal rest. You left me to do hard labour as a child, serving out my sentence, even though I had committed no crime. I understand, Mama, but it's still hard. I knew you couldn't afford to keep me – your salary so bare, so little – but I wish you had kept me. I wish you had chosen to raise me. But you had no choice, and I understand that. Will I have a choice? My boy was on The Farm. I don't want him to go back. To take him there in the first place was so hard, but what was I supposed to do? I gave birth to him there at that place…and to put him there again for four weeks that August was not easy. Not many people knew what it was, but I do… what we were being treated like. It was so heartbreaking to see and hear the stories – we are not treated like human beings. Papa, Mama, I had to leave my boy there at that horrible place, with Survival not a given. I close my eyes. Nothing besides barely enough food, water… it could never be enough in a place like that. I am trying to get him out. He is in care, treated as a pauper, with people I don't know. I don't know how he is doing, but I am doing what I can… I don't know when I'll see him again, when I'll be able to hold him in my arms and tell him that everything is going to be all right… It   is   so   hard.

Time is slipping, going through the hourglass, sifting, shifting, disappearing… I am now in quicksand. What do I do? But, somehow, I am here with the Mystical ones, including the Snow Queene. Somehow, light has shone – an archway of light – and as I walked through, it took me to these women, including the daughters of Mother Mnemosyne. I never thought…

And I am of the line going back to Mother Mnemosyne. I am also of the line of those who built the Akan empire… I am of both worlds – I am of many worlds – this is what they are telling me. That's what my Mama told me, and my Papa, to remember both worlds. And now in this land, which is more than one land, that influences as far as Tír na nÓg… I see. Yes, I do see. But, Papa, I do my best for my boy.

I hope that I can get him free, give him the flight of emancipation. Even though he was born free, he will still have to fight for opportunity. I don't want him to live in squalor and extreme subsistence. He is waiting for me, but they see him as a person with no value. Brigid, Protector of all Storytellers, and Mother Mnemosyne, help me to continue to move on, push on, through – for my son, for me, for all of us who are on the precipice, because of the colour of our skin.

Chapter Twelve:
Memory

HERE it is – Story… Here It – The Dragon was black, standing proud, with a red aura around her. "I am here. You have not known me in your lifetime, but through your magic, being the great-great-great-granddaughter of Mother Mnemosyne, you see me."

Somehow, I knew – she was the Guardian. She protected the city of London. I had read about the Great Fire, about Christopher Wren and how he rebuilt The Temple Bar – made it bigger for carriageways – yes, made it... Yes, I remembered. I had access to books because of the family I worked for. And so, because of my papyrical friends, I did Remember.

I remembered the temple gate that he built; it was facing me. In my memories, I remembered. I remembered how the monarch had to greet the city mayor to gain entrance into the City. I remembered the illustrations and descriptions about London that I had read in books I could get from the Hayward's family library – doing so in secret. And so, I remembered seeing another of Wren's creations – Christchurch Grey Friars, the magnificent steeple, one of Coventry's three spires...

I remembered The Royal Hospital For Seamen at Greenwich – the buildings, the blue towers, the black wrought iron gates with gold, and I remember standing at a building – red brick, Portland stone… a lady's face peeking out at me, and columns that reminded me of the ones built by the Greeks. Through the power of books, I remember walking around the gardens and seeing the Thames. I remember. I think about Christopher Wren – his achievements firmly in my memories, as if forged in brick and stone. I think of all these things. I think of all these things. I remember fountains, parks... I remember, I Remember.

And seeing you, the great dragon, you emblazoned in black – it all comes back. You are from a different Time, a Time that has Not Yet Come To Pass. Yes, I still see you because of The One, The Mystical One who had ten daughters, all part of a Mystical Circle. With a vermilion aura, through Space and Time, I see you and your Sisters, emblazoned in silver metallic with red, the shields standing proud... A Coal Exchange... These words come into my mind even though it's not of my time, but as the great-great-great-granddaughter of Mother Mnemosyne, I have the gift of forethought and precognition – I am remembering, I am swimming through past, present, and future. Yes, I remember Your Sisters – the Silver ones greet me, and I bow to them – they are the Guardians, guarding not only the treasures of London, but guarding the treasures that are memories. The dragon nodded.

Yes, I'm the Memory, as I am the great-great-great-granddaughter of Mother Mnemosyne, the Goddess of Memory. My aunts have told me. Yes, my Aunts. So much to tell, so much to explore. Now, I must rest, for another adventure awaits in this great city. I am seeing so many things that will not come to pass yet: a gold eagle overlooking the Thames, a great bridge with a pair of towers and ensconced in blue, and a clock in a clock tower that rings sonorously to proclaim freedom, welcome, and timelessness. Again, these things have not yet come to pass, but I see them in my mind's eye. I am remembering something else: a book, an edition to be published in this Magical City, a city founded by the Romans – Londinium... This book – is it connected to me? I wonder.

Waves of memories wash over me now. Yes, they wash over me. I must now continue to Dream, to be in the land of Waking dreams. For we dream not just during the evening hours, but also when we are awake, and those dreamers – those artists – that is when they also reach a place, a work of the finest hours. The importance of Dreaming. To Dream, To Dream,

To DREAM.

The black dragon spoke. "Immerging. Synergy. Unity. You, you seek… Wholeness... Who are you? You seek your origins; you seek your genesis. Listen to the voice in your head. Listen to the voice in your heart – the sweet music, the sweet music. Yes, Harriet. Yes, Harriet. That is what you seek."

I then saw a lion by the river, a lion of white; he was the guardian. I saw again the eagle of gold that also overlooked this river, murky in her depths – an eagle that watched over everything. Watched over… Watched over… Her wings ready to soar into flight. A cathedral with many tombs, and the sound of peaceful silence – a meditation – that surrounded people with waves of tranquility. I heard this, I saw this... It was as if I knew – as if it was something that

I would know. Yes, yes, yes. Dreams of Memory, swirls of thought, sound, and voice. I was Remembering – but has it happened yet? I was trying to remember. And the book, this book that would be forged in this Londinium… How is it connected to me? Would I know? Would I discover what the answer is? Was This The Stuff Of Dreams? Was it? Or was I crossing over into Something Else?

Chapter Thirteen:
Cara Is Dreamwalking

I am asleep, but somehow, I feel that I am awake. A dragon has come to me – a huge black one with a red aura surrounding her. She is majestic, but somehow not intimidating – her eyes a bright hazel.

"It is time, Dear one, Youngling. It is time to Dream. Come." I followed her through a gate shining with emeralds and rubies. I was in a garden. Then, I passed through some columns. I faced a red brick building, with a woman's face peering out from its walls. "Are you ready, Cara?" asked the dragon. I nodded. She smiled.

I was lifted up, up, into the air, and there I found myself in a city of gold and velvet. Castles with turrets of emerald glimmer from a distance. I saw a bridge – a towered one – ensconced in purple. I drifted into one of the doors of the bridge, and inside I was surrounded by books, tomes really, and another dragon, a guardian gleaming silver, red, and white with a shield and a sword.

"Come," she said. "Come, this way." I nodded and followed her. There was a clearing, and the sky was punctuated with bright stars, gleaming silver, gold, and amaranth.

"It must begin," the dragon said. "It Must." I saw a

window in front of me, and I looked in. I then walked into the frame and saw woods and a castle. "Yes," the dragon whispered. "That is where it must begin."

There were three princesses, and the King was concerned that they would not get married. He set each of them a task. He said, "Take this harp. Play with all your might, and any who has an eagle come to her, that one will marry." The three daughters played on harps of gold, and two eagles came and sat at a stool near two of his daughters – the two oldest. The eagles then turned into men, and they were overjoyed. The two would be married in a fortnight. The third played with all her might, but no eagle came. Suddenly, a swan flew in and looked at the third daughter. She loved swans, but how would that help her find a mate, a husband?

She was still grateful for the gift, for Karena was not to be easily disappointed, happy with her lot in life. She was a princess, after all. So, she still happily accepted the swan. The two eldest daughters went to court, presenting their future husbands, and for the rest of the family to meet them. The third was always greeted with the gentle smile of the King, as he loved all his daughters but had a special fondness in his heart for the third, because she always exuded kindness in every situation and sought to see the beauty in everyone. She often helped those who were disadvantaged, reading to and teaching the poor, whereas the other two daughters were not interested. The third daughter made sure no one went hungry and consulted with the advisors in the kingdom to make sure that there was enough in the reserves for all to have food. The King supported her in that and other endeavours to make the world a better place. He always stood up for her, even when the eldest daughters treated her badly or ignored her. Yes, he loved all of his girls, but would not tolerate ignorance or ill will.

The King said to the youngest, "Go forth to your chambers. Bring the swan, and later, the maid will come for it and put it in the stables. It will be all right. You will learn a lot from this sweet creature. Mother Nature is the best teacher."

The daughter nodded and took the swan to her chambers. She would often read to it, and the swan seemed to listen. One day, she took the swan to the river, singing to it, and the swan seemed to listen to every note. She started reading a fairy tale to the swan by the river. The swan sat and seemed to listen intently.

People at court told the princess to name the swan, but she would not relent. She replied, "No, the name of this swan is simply Swan, and that will do." The princess was not interested in making matters complicated. Life was too short for these frivolities. She filled her days with reading, going to the river with Swan by her side. One afternoon, as she continued to read to the swan, a shimmer of light surrounded the creature. The creature started to float over the river.

The princess was at first alarmed, but then the swan spoke and said, "Don't be afraid. All is well, and I will not do you any harm." Then, the swan suddenly disappeared. He reappeared, and there he was – a HE! The swan had become a man. Karena was shocked. The swan... was... a man.

"Don't be concerned, Karena. I am the same, but different. I am a shape-shifter, that is my nature, like the Others from the line Verandaes. I am here, as was wished by your father, to be your husband. Would that be your heart's desire?" Karena nodded. "Well, then that is how it should be – that is how it will be. Come, Karena, I will meet your father."

Then, Karena became afraid – what if her father wouldn't accept her new husband, who all this time was a Swan? She told her future husband about her concerns.

"All right, then," said the young man, with dark, jet-black hair and blue eyes. "I will only appear to you as human until you are ready to tell your father." The princess nodded.

The King was happy for his first two daughters – the third, he was concerned about, but felt she was too young to marry anyway, and that she could remain as she was, enjoying life as a princess. The father asked the husbands of the first two to fetch him a goose for dinner. The first two tried but failed. The young daughter asked if she could help. The King agreed. She talked to her beau. He, in his human form, went into the forest to hunt and brought back a goose.

He gave it to the princess, and she gave it to her father. The father was impressed. "Yes, this is delightful," he said at that evening's dinner.

Then, he asked for a golden egg from a magical duck – a Vaaksim – as the yolk from these golden eggs was useful in strengthening the drawbridge and the walls around the kingdom, as the golden yolk was used as mortar to strengthen structures. The two husbands did as they were told but couldn't procure a golden egg. The young princess asked her suitor to procure an egg; he did so and gave it to the princess. She then gave it to the King, and again he was pleased. He did not ask how his youngest got these things, but he felt that in time, she would tell him.

The princess and her suitor were happy. The princess had him live in a separate tower, and she would visit from time to time. But she did not feel good about keeping this secret and so had decided to tell her father. That was to be the way. There was to be a ball. The King wanted to celebrate the marriages of his two oldest daughters and the plucky feistiness of his youngest that made it possible to get the things he requested, these things which the first two could not.

The eldest daughters were suspicious and sought to find out how the daughter was getting these things, such as the golden egg. One of the sisters found out, from a maid, that the youngest princess was spending a lot of time in another tower, separate from the rest of the castle. She followed the princess to this chamber and saw her talking to a man. She was shocked. She would talk to their father and tell him. She rushed down the stairs. The ball was about to begin, and the King was busy talking to traders about the state of affairs, the coffers of the Kingdom, and couldn't be found. The Queen was also busy with preparations for the ball that was about to begin – some last-minute decisions had to be made about meals and so on. It was a lot to organize. With clinking glasses, silverware, plates, and chandeliers that still had to be cleaned, all on the day of the ball, the eldest princess couldn't reach her mother either to tell her about the princess' secret. "But mother and father will know about this," she thought. Vioneya vowed to get this secret out.

The youngest princess had no idea about what was to happen – she and her intended – because they knew that in their hearts, their company solely involved reading, books, discussing literature, the arts, science, and astronomy; all the things the other princesses did not show any interest in. Karena and her intended would often hold hands during their time together, and that was enough for the princess. The young man respected her wishes. For when it was time, they would tell her father, and hopefully, get his blessing. If not, the princess vowed, they would elope, because she was determined to hold on to this happiness no matter what, for life was too short to waste it on trifles, protocols, or pretense. That is what she told her intended – her Heart. They decided to go to the ball together. She left for her chamber, and her love stayed in his and got ready.

He put on his finest tunic, looking so handsome. The princess wore her prettiest gown, ice blue with puffy sleeves and a dress that fanned out like a bell. It was the same colour as the bell at the village church in the kingdom. She went down to the ball. Her intended followed. The ballroom was aglow with mirrors, music, velvet walls ensconced with marble, and chandeliers of elven crystal. Karena's intended walked to the ballroom floor. The princess came to his side, and they danced, danced, and danced. Images of rivers, unicorns, and emerald forests came into the eyes of whoever was looking at the handsome couple.

The other two sisters were amiss. They thought to themselves, "Who is this man?" But the eldest then remembered and said out loud, "This man, he is –"

Then, out of nowhere, there appeared a dragon and a griffin. They stormed through the ballroom, stepping on anything that got in their way. The guests were horrified, seeing people trampled to death. The intended of the princess closed his eyes, and in his hands appeared a sword and shield made out of elven silver, the handle glimmering with rubies, emeralds, and amethysts. He rose into the air and started fighting the beasts. He chopped the head off one and stabbed the other, the griffin, who quickly disappeared in a puff of pink smoke. The dragon then disappeared as well, moments after his head dropped to the ground, almost killing another person – Karena, thinking quickly, had run to push that person out of the way, who she then discovered to be her oldest sister. The sister smiled gratefully at the youngest.

The King gathered everyone around to reassure them that everything would be all right, that no one else would come to harm. He then spoke to the young man. "I am grateful for what you have done." He smiled. "I am grateful, and you… I don't know you, but somehow, I feel like I do. Explain, young man."

The young man, with hair like the night and eyes of an unforgettable azure, spoke. "I have to be forthcoming, Your Highness. I am not what you think I am, but I also am. I was the swan that came to the side of your youngest when she played on the harp. Her music called to me because it represented her kindness and resourcefulness in a world where these things are not quite valued in a human being, never mind a young woman. She is a princess after all, but as you know, some in royalty are not kind, thinking they are better than others solely because of royal blood. I do not think that is right and deem it not to be so. Someone's heart – their soul – is the true worth of a person, man or woman. I apologize for keeping this secret. Your daughter –"

The princess joined in. "Papa, I was afraid that you would not accept our union, as he was a swan, for quite some time, until recently. Only a fortnight ago did he reveal himself to me. But I should not have kept it a secret, not even then. I am truly sorry. I accept all responsibility and any punishment you wish to give."

"Daughter, I am saddened that you thought I would judge your intended." The princess continued to look at her father, a serious expression in her hazel eyes. "I do, though, understand. These things, these mysteries – sometimes it's hard to have faith that others will understand. But in future, know that I will believe all that you say. You are an honourable young woman, Karena, and have a huge heart, kindness, and a capacity for compassion. Do not think that because I am ruler of this land that I would not see as you do. Remember." Karena nodded her head vigorously, with a beaming look in her eyes. "You do love him, I know, and I already see respect and a sense of propriety. Words. Ideas. I know that those were the things that were shared: a love of books, knowledge, and as the person – the woman – I raised you to be, I know that was all… the sharing of hearts, connections, and interests in different worlds, and that was all that was to pass." The princess nodded.

"Yes, as I knew it to be, that is how I raised you. I have also let others," he said, looking at the other two daughters, "carry on in a way not fitting for princesses – being unkind, selfish, and treating others with a lack of dignity and respect. Even towards you, Karena. I did intervene at times, but I should have done more. I should not have allowed any of that to carry on at all. I am sorry too. For if I had stopped that entirely, you would have been more comfortable telling me all this."

The princess nodded again, with tears in her eyes. "Yes, Papa, I forgive you. It's all right. And forgive me for not telling you sooner about me and Conaen."

"It's not all right, what I did," said the King solemnly.

"But I accept your apology wholeheartedly, as you have accepted mine. Let us now forget about this and have a moment of silence for those who have passed, for somehow, their bodies have disappeared into nothingness."

"That is the way, when The Bergantaes encounter human beings," said Conaen quietly. He added, "There is Death, then nothingness. No bloodshed, no remnants of rotting flesh – that is their way."

The King nodded. A moment of silence had begun, and then it was decided to continue with the ball in memorial to those who had passed and to celebrate the future. So, the ball continued. But then, another creature appeared – it was a red dragon, even larger than the first, and took one swipe at the young man whose name was Conaen. The dragon was stopped by an emerald cloud that surrounded Conaen, as he sensed danger almost right away. But the red dragon murmured something... in hushed tones. The emerald cloud disappeared, and he grabbed the young man. Karena looked on, petrified. She cried, screaming, "No... Noooooo!!!" The dragon and her love disappeared in a cloud of silver dust.

"Fear not, child," shouted the King. "We will find him." The youngest was in tears. The eldest daughters, especially the oldest, embraced Karena.

"He will be found," she said quietly. "We will not give up."

The King sent his sentinels traversing different worlds, as he knew of the Teranicus who were descendants of King Arthur. They went forth. Men, and yes, women, outfitted in silver armour forged by a very skilled tribe of elves. These knights could go backwards and forwards through time. But to no avail. Conaen was not found. The princess cried for one hundred days and one hundred nights. The king did not know what to do. His wife, the Queen, was at a loss for words. She felt helpless.

"Augus," she whispered. "Our girl, our youngest – she is not well. What can we do? We have not found him. We are all out of sorts, and I do not know what to say or what to suggest. You have called for the old wise woman who lives just outside our gates?"

"Yes, but there is no answer. She has not been found. I don't know what to make of it. Usually, she responds when I put out the call, the request for help."

The two didn't know what to do. The Kingdom was affected. The princess usually took food from banquets and so on to the poor, and she had read to disadvantaged kids and taught them how to read and write. But with her in such grief, those whom she helped were at a loss as well. The other two daughters stepped in and did their best, but they could not be a substitute for the kindness, compassion, and empathy of their youngest sister. The children would often ask for her and were concerned, upset that their princess was enshrouded in sadness. And so, she retreated into herself in a tower in the west wing, not far from where she would go and talk to her intended about the love of books, literature, science, the stars, the cosmos, and astronomy... She loved these things, but no longer, as she was experiencing dark days. No one knew what to do.

One day, a faerie with crystal wings and enrobed in velvet appeared to the princess. "Princess," she said, "you must not despair. You have the Power."

"No, I don't," sobbed the princess. "My father's army couldn't find him. I tried to help the squires, looking at maps, suggesting where they should go to find him, suggesting different worlds, but it was all amiss. I don't know what to do. I am helpless."

"No, you are not," said the faerie. "You have the power. You know what to do. To find your future – to fight for it – you have to do it yourself. You are The Key."

"But I am a princess."

"Is that all that you are? Do we not have more than one gift, more than one skill? More than one path?"

Karena thought for a moment, "I never saw it that way."

"You must. Forge your path, one of many different gifts, many different destinies – we all have more than one blessing to give to the world. Find out what your gifts are. Find out who you are. And from there, everything else will Spring. Everything else will come forward. You must if your future is to be realized."

The princess nodded and then set out on a Journey to find her Beloved. She told her father and mother, and even though they both had reservations, they gave her their blessing as they could not let their daughter continue to be immersed in sadness and melancholy. That was not the way of the world or of a life. No. The father, the King, went into a chest of oak and brought her three things: a dagger, a sword, and a globe of glass. "These things will help you on your journey."

The mother also nodded. "And this," the mother added, for she had her blacksmith make this in anticipation of any who would set out to find the intended of her youngest. It was armour of elvish silver and gold, with mother-of-pearl and amethysts that dotted the helmet and arms and legs of the suit of armour. The princess gasped. The mother said, "It is your time." She then smiled. "It is your time to be who you are meant to be. I love you so much. You are a joy like our other two, but you always had a kindness, a heart to help those in trouble and in need. We did not tell you – we adopted you from the wise woman who lives outside our gates. She came to us – she found a babe in the woods, a babe who had lost her parents. She brought you to us. She knew somehow that there was a connection – that you would be on the right path with our love and guidance. She told us. And we agreed and raised you as our own. We love all of our girls, we never played favourites, but your heart always shone through – you always wanted to help others. You always advocated for what was right. When there were those who were hungry or needed to learn, you stepped in, unlike the other two. Yes, we love all of our girls – we treated you all equally – but we always had a fondness and a deep respect for you for what you have done. Things that were not necessary, above the call of duty. I tell you this: you should be proud of who you are! But you must also find out what your Story is, and maybe, by seeking to find your intended, you will find the Story of your Beginnings, of your genesis. I know you understand." The princess just nodded and hugged them both.

Outfitted with this suit of armour, sword, shield, and the globe of glass that shone like a rainbow, which the King put in a velvet pouch, she was on the way with enough supplies for a year and a day. She had a horse – Serkaenasis – a fine steed descended from Pegasus, who would have wings to escape any danger or to get to an intended destination even faster. Karena was grateful for this, and she set out at dawn. She galloped through forests, jumped over drystone walls, met other faerie folk and mortals, and went through villages until she came to a mountain. She flew up the mountain with Serkaenasis as she gleamed in shades of magenta, gold, and ivory. She rose to the top of the mountain thanks to her wings, which appeared out of nowhere. The mystical steed circled the mountain, looking to see if there was any danger. Seeing none, she descended onto the icy mountain top. There was a cottage on top of the mountain, a thatched-roof cottage. It appeared out of sorts with the icy mountain landscape, but that's what it was. Karena jumped down from the steed. She told Serkaenasis, "Stay here. If there is any danger, I'll let you know. If it becomes too dangerous for you, leave. Leave without me. I do not want you to be hurt."

"I await your instructions, dear Princess," replied the steed with eyes of sparkling viridian. "Yes, I await your instructions. I will be on the lookout."

"Thank you, Sister," Karena replied. "Thank you."

She walked toward the thatched cottage and opened the door of oak, painted vermilion, a half circle. She walked inside. It was filled with Light. She continued. There were passageways, tunnels, and she walked toward another door of amethyst. She opened it. Karena went inside. She gasped – it was like the universe was opening up, a black sky dotted with stars, nebulae, and so on. She was entranced. Where was she? She really did not know.

"Karena," said a voice, weakly. She looked to the right. There was her beloved, but he was tied to a dying star whose embers were slowly fading out. "Be careful. He is here. The –"

Behind Karena was a lion – a lion with wings and fangs of gold. "You are here, here at last," he said grimly. "It's time. Face me if you want your beloved. You'll have to kill me."

Karena nodded. She nodded again, vigorously. "I am ready," she said quietly. "I am at The Ready."

The lion stepped down from his pedestal of marble. "Let us begin."

Instinctively, Karena raised her hands towards the roof of the cavern. Slowly, her body rose into the air, and suddenly, she was face to face with the lion. He swiped at her. She quickly dodged him. He swiped again, but again, he missed his target. He breathed fire, emanating shades of scarlet, indigo, and gold, but Karena then closed her eyes, and a cloud of emerald surrounded her, protecting her from the flames.

"You are a Garanshee," he smiled. "I never thought I would meet one in this lifetime. You are the Only One. You are the Last One of your line. Are you prepared to die?"

"I will do whatever it takes to have my Beloved back with me in my arms. I will do whatever is necessary."

"Well then, child, prepare for the end... Prepare –"

He closed his eyes, and the whole chamber shook. Spikes of ice came down from the ceiling of the cavern, barely missing her intended, but Conaen was able to create a forcefield of gold to protect himself. Karena did the same, but her orb was blue – a deep aquamarine – and protected her from harm as well.

"The Garanshee," he sneered. "No, I will not have it. You will die."

He then turned into a scorpion and, with his claws, started to scratch at the blue orb. Karena closed her eyes and heard The Call of her people like a chorus of voices, harmonic voices raised in song. Karena continued. No, she would not be deterred from her Destiny.

The scorpion then became a cobra. Then the

shape-shifter from the line Jurgantean became a leopard with wings and started to claw at the orb of aquamarine. Karena would not relent. She would have her destiny.

Then, the creature turned into a likeness of her father. Karena was taken aback. She gasped. "Father?"

"Karena," shouted Conaen, her love. "That is not him. Do not be fooled. Stay strong – focus. Stay strong."

Unfortunately, the princess was so taken aback that the orb became weak. The leopard clawed his way through, striking the princess. Blood started to seep from between the gaps in her armour and chainmail. The winged leopard struck again, and more blood fell onto the floor of quartz.

"Karena, stay strong. Remember who you are!" Conaen shouted again.

The princess was at a loss. "Was that Papa?" She couldn't understand, until a vision of the old woman whom she didn't quite remember, but somehow...

"Karena, Remember: You are descended from the line Garanshee. Strike back, be strong – Remember, And Embrace Who You ARE."

The princess, hearing those words and seeing the image of that woman, opened up her eyes. She had nearly been put into a deep sleep, as the winged leopard had an intoxicating venom in his claws that put people into a deep slumber. Karena woke up and jumped into action. She had the sword, but the leopard was immersed in a black cloud. She took the glass globe that appeared in her hand and used it as a beacon. She started to fly toward the cloud, which was now revealed to be the leopard with wings, and the sword appeared in her left hand, as she was ambidextrous. She took the sword and threw it at the Beast. The eyes started to glow red, and he screamed, "NO...!!!" He then shrieked, his screams shaking the walls of the cavern. Karena then conjured up some daggers with ruby and amethyst handles, and along with the dagger given to her by her father, threw them at the beast – right into his eyes and also into his chest, where his heart was. He continued to scream and then started to moan – a horrible, unforgettable howl. The princess would not relent.

"I am from the line Garanshee. I will not give up –" She drew a large sword – the one given to her by her father, which had never been seen before and was a sword from the Mystical Ones, the Tuatha Dé Dannan, who came from across the sea – and Karena threw it at the beast. Somehow, she was also connected to the Celts and the Tuatha Dé Danann, as all the mystical beings, gods, goddesses, and magical tribes were connected one way or another in a circle of Mystical strength and power.

"Be Gone!" Karena screamed. "Be GONE!" The winged leopard changed back into a cobra, then a scorpion, and finally changed back into a lion with wings as he continued to scream, blood spurting everywhere. "You will be Gone. Evil, Be Gone, NOW!"

A Burst of Bright White Light Shot Forth and blasted through the lion. He screamed again, and then, silence. He was gone. Only bits of ash fell down to the quartz floor of this cavern, a tunnel fixed in Time.

"You did it." Conaen smiled. "You did it! Yes, you did it!" He cheered from below. Suddenly, out of nowhere, came faeries from different parts of the world, including the Aziza from the land of desert, sycamore trees, the savannah, and the Sphinx... another long mystical line. Shouts in unison rose up to greet the princess, still suspended in the air. "You have done it!" shouted the future prince. "You have done it! Now, you know who you are! I always believed."

The princess smiled with tears of joy. She descended from the depths of the air to meet her Beloved. They embraced each other. They embraced. "I am so happy I found you; I am happy beyond words. I feel such joy." Karena added, "My Heart, are you okay?"

"Yes, I am now. I am," said Conaen, sighing. "You – I am so proud of you. And I will be proud to be your husband; I cannot wait until we are wed."

Karena nodded. "Yes. Papa and Mama will be pleased. They will be happy that I found you, and that you are all right."

"They will also be happy that you now know who you are," said the young man quietly. "I have known for quite some time, and that is one of the reasons why I answered the Call. I knew you were one of the Garanshee, and I wanted to meet you, to know you. Yes, I didn't know you were the last of your line, but your ancestors, they are known for their bravery, kindness, and compassion. For those reasons, I had to seek you out."

The princess nodded. Yes, she was happy – so happy. She talked to the other faeriekind who were also imprisoned in this cavern carved into the mountain. Conaen tried to save them but was punished by being tied to the dying star. They were at a loss for what to do, but Conaen said help was coming. They asked how he knew. He just said that he did. One of the Aziza proclaimed, "Your Beloved has another sense; he knows. He knew you would come." Karena looked at Conaen with his jet-black hair and deep blue eyes that met her chestnut ones.

"Yes, Karena, I did," he said. "I knew you would come.

You are so unlike your other sisters and many I have met. You are driven by justice and a sense of compassion, to do what's right, and willing to sacrifice your life for others. At the ball, and even now, I have seen. That is another reason why I sought you out. I knew. And I am so happy that you'll be my wife. We were meant to be together, for all Time."

The princess smiled and embraced her Beloved; they kissed. The faeries all smiled, clapped, and cheered, for that was the first time their lips touched. The two said goodbye to their new friends and invited them all to the wedding. If they wanted to return with them to their kingdom, they were welcome. Some joined them, others went back to their respective homes and would join them later for the wedding and celebration. Some of the Aziza joined them. When the couple went through the doorway of the cottage and walked toward Sarkaenasis, she smiled.

"It went well, didn't it?" She said, laughing.

"You know... You know everything?" asked Karena, surprised, but thought she shouldn't be, as Sarkaenasis was also from a mystical line.

"I am descended from the line of Pegasus – we know these things." She laughed again. "I knew you could do it. You do have The Power, as you are from the line Garanshee. It is wonderful to see you again, Conaen," Sarkaenasis nodded at the young man. "I am happy that you are relatively unscathed."

"Thanks to my intended, yes," said Conaen with a smile. "Let us go, Karena. Let us go back to your kingdom, the realm of Dergantaes." Sarkaenasis nodded her head. Karena smiled, and the couple hopped onto the steed's back. They travelled through different worlds, through

Space and Time, until they entered the realm of Dergantaes. The King and Queen were so happy to see their daughter and their future son-in-law.

"Yes," said the King, "I had always believed." He then gave her a big hug.

The Queen followed. "My daughter, there are just not the words… You have made us so proud, yet again. And your Sisters – they see what I see, and they are following suit, following your example. They have been teaching the young ones, teaching them how to read and write while you've been away. They are learning, slowly, because of you. Yes, we are so proud." The princess smiled.

Her two sisters came and embraced her. The oldest sister apologized. "I was wrong to want to spite you, to expose a secret that was of no consequence. For even then, you acted honourably."

"That is my way," said Karena simply with a warmth in her eyes.

"I know. I realize that you had reservations about how Papa would feel about Conaen, and that is the only reason why you did what you did. I understand. Forgive me for my jealousy."

"I do," said the younger sister. "It is all forgiven. Let us now celebrate the Joy Of Life." They all came together and celebrated.

The wedding happened in a fortnight. After the ceremony that was attended from far and wide – from the lands of the pyramids and the Sphinx to the druids from the lands of green and mist...and from many other worlds – they gathered in Celebration of The One who was brave, fought for justice, compassion, and most of all, Love. It was the spark that had united all worlds. This would never be forgotten. No. No. No.

***

And so, I, Cara, now proclaimed guardian of Harriet E. Wilson, saw this and was watching all of it unfold. I stepped back from the window framed in gold and velvet.

The dragon looked at me. "Do you see?"

"I don't know," I said softly.

"Yes, you do," insisted the dragon. "Respect, dignity, and compassion, but also a sense of what is right, what has to be done... and Love. It is all there. You do see. You think you do not, but you do see." I nodded.

"My mother – why? Why isn't she the Guardian, the Protector of the One to Unite All Worlds?"

"We all have our Path. And it involves different gifts, different blessings. One person's path is not another's. Your mother's path is different from yours. You are a warrior of the line Jeyagentis. That is part of who you are, but you are not just that, for we are many parts of ourselves because of our different gifts. You will know what your gifts are, and you will know your path."

"How?" I asked.

"By walking it. Walk The Path, Cara. Walk The Path – that is how you'll know. Walk THE PATH." I nodded. "Yes, it is time. Soon, The Messenger must walk into another realm so that her work will get out into many Worlds, including a world called Londinium – a place established by the Romans, a world with dragons, a wall, bridges... And a river, The Thames, and a monarch, but most importantly, someone who will publish her words. Her words must get out into All Worlds; you will have to guide her, Cara, and be her Protector. For this next Journey might be rough. You have to be up to that Task. Do you know what to do?"

"I have to Walk The Path."

"Yes, and by Walking it, you will Know It. Walk It. Know It. Forge It, Forge The Path in Glory and Bravery. It is your TIME."

I nodded again, and the Tuatha Dé Danann appeared, along with druids – some were women of colour, as many of the druid lines accepted women to be leaders and spiritual teachers. The Celts nodded. "She is Remembering, and she will know who she is."

"Yes," said the Goddess of Poetry, Brigid, her cousin being Tuerini, the Great-Great-Great-Grandmother Of Harriet and Twin sister of Euterpe. Yes...   And there was another... A man robed in silk and velvet, whose mirror brother was residing in a stained-glass window... in a monastery framed by the Shehy Mountains.

"Yes, Yes, Yes..." said Saint Fin Barre. "More will come to pass."

The two women connected to the Tuatha Dé Danann also agreed, and so did Anisie, still Queen of the Spider World but now having full agency as she could shape-shift into being a spider at any time, but if she stayed in that form for too long, she would remain as a spider. All the Immortals nodded.

I, Cara, walked back to the palace, sometimes still not believing what I had seen, what I had experienced. I had just woken up after the Dream and had to get some fresh evening air. The dragon was real. The Dream was real. They were all calling to me: The Mystical Ones from across The Ages. Something was happening. Something magical and miraculous – it was a sign of more to come.

As I came down the circular staircase, I saw Selena,

a compatriot of Anisie, the Spider Queen. I noticed that Selena also felt something. Was she thinking that my mom, Kerianna, still in the other world in a city north of the 49th parallel, the first one to enter a different world – sensed something? I wondered, too, as it felt like I had been gone for quite some time. It was only six hours in my mom's world, my gut instinct told me, but in this one, it was six weeks. But did my mom sense that something was wrong, or did she know deep down that I was being looked after and protected? I wondered, and looking into Selena's inquisitive eyes, I knew she felt the same way. There was no way I could reach my mother from this world, but I tried to let her know in letters I could never send, and in my heart, by just closing my eyes and thinking about her, that I was okay. Somehow, I knew that it would be enough. Somehow, I knew.

Harriet was still residing with the Snow Queene for the most part but would venture into the other world where she lived, in Boston, momentarily, to not raise suspicion. But really, she preferred to stay with her mystical friends and those connected to her mother, and she now had met all of her aunts, those who were daughters of Mother Mnemosyne. She had not yet met Mother Mnemosyne, her great-great-great-grandmother, but soon would… Harriet had a feeling.

The Aunts were happy to see Harriet and to know that she was doing well. They knew that their Sister had a daughter who had to be hidden away from danger and was later adopted into an Ashanti tribe. Of course, that baby was Harriet's great-grandmother, Dhakirah. It was wonderful to see Harriet so happy. I had a feeling her life in Boston was not so joyful, and she just needed a break from that world, which could be harsh and cruel, especially toward a woman of colour. All of her great Aunts knew that and taught Harriet about the different gifts they had to bestow. They also talked about Homer, Shakespeare, and all the other masters from that classical area of literature. All the Sisters, especially Calliope, the Muse Of Poetry, knew the original Greek texts, and also the literature of the gods and goddesses they themselves created on Mount Olympus, where Zeus ruled. They taught Harriet all about this, their beloved great-great-grand-niece. Harriet felt so loved. They said that her life, her role as a Messenger, would be very important. They said not to take credence in those who looked down on her because of who she was. Tears rolled down her cheek, her face that had a beautiful tone of mocha. They said, in the end, it would not matter, for her words would forge through time as she was the Chosen One.

There were Others, yes, with other gifts, and those similar to hers, but never quite what she had, as there was no copy – no replica – in their world or in the world of Mortals. A human being was unique, for all time. They told Harriet this. No one could ever be her. No one. Only she could tell her Story.

Harriet felt comforted. Harriet felt loved. She felt like she belonged somewhere and was grateful. Her novel was coming fast, even faster than the poetry she wrote but never published, except for one poem. This work was being called, was being beckoned – it needed to be published. They told her it would be done – not to be despondent. They embraced and loved her and gave Harriet support and comfort. Yes, they did. And so, the Story continued. And I, Cara, was happy to be a part of this story. And so, the Story, for all of us, would never end. It would ring through time, and that was true not just for Harriet, but for all of us, as we are all connected – part of a chain, part of the same Story, for Story united us all.

Chapter Fourteen:
Cara Is The Guardian

THE water, a magical golden stream of the Organic. We were there on a bench, not far from the lions on Centre Street Bridge, as we were now were in Calgary, the city with the Lions… I remembered that the bridge was inspired by the lion statues in Trafalgar Square. I had been there before in London. But I remember a man admonishing – no, berating – his daughter. He slapped her... the woman, the mother, was mortified, and I didn't know what to do... The world was not what it was supposed to be. The lions looked on, but I imagined in my mind's eye that they came alive, jumped off their pedestals, and tore the man to shreds. That was in my mind's eye. When I walked across the Centre Street Bridge with people before and behind us, that's what I thought.

The Snow Queene, Eberveen, along with Anisie and Stargette, had decided that I, Cara, should come along with Harriet, being her Guardian and Protector to this other world. Here, Harriet would discover more about herself and what she had to do to be The Messenger to save all worlds. They had also decided that Oceantis, the tall woman with pink hair, should come with me, as well as her friend and cousin, Staerkie, the younger woman with blue hair and inquisitive purple eyes. Selena wanted to stay behind, looking over all the parchment, scrolls, and books made of leather and gold to find out more about the Darkness that was coming. Stargette had also decided to remain, protecting not only Selena, but also the Snow Queene and her lair. There was also a discussion with Brigid, the Protector of all Storytellers. Brigid had decided that she also must remain, for now, to figure out a strategy to protect all worlds, including the land of the Snow Queene, Tír na nÓg, and any other mystical realms. Brigid would be in contact with the others, including the Tuatha Dé Danann, as she knew that an Army would have to be formed. An Army of Light would sear through and pierce the Darkness that would come. She knew that they had to be At The Ready. And so they would be, in time.

I thought about all that strategizing that would have to take place, and shivers went down my spine. Would we be ready? And what enemies would we be facing? It was hard to know at this time, in this time and space. But the lions on this bridge reminded me that we are more connected than we think – by ideas, by memory. I saw something in the distance; it was a statue of an ibis. Anisie saw it, too, and motioned us to go over. When we were closer, Anisie touched it. She then said, "They are expecting us."

As soon as we were closer together, our feet were lifted off the ground, and we flew, flew, flew, and then we saw it – the gold dancing on the water, the Golden Organic on the Bow River. We got closer to the water's edge, and I was scared that we would fall in, but Anisie said, "No, don't be afraid."

I nodded, still paralyzed with fear. I did have a fear of

heights. Well, just a fear of… of what I didn't know, what I didn't understand. We got closer to the water's edge, and then there was silence. And then, there was more Silence. And then –

In front of me was a different shade of Light… It was softer. In front of me were columns. We walked down the stairs, and there was a light like an old-fashioned lantern above us. I kept walking. There was a tall building of red brick and stone. Up, up – I had to strain my neck – there were two faces… Women's faces… Facades of stone. They were looking down at us. I looked at Harriet, but she just smiled, as if she knew what was about to happen next. But how? I looked back at the woman's face made out of stone. Anisie smiled at all of us, then turned and said, "We are ready."

One of the stone faces nodded. Suddenly, there was a chasm, an opening in the courtyard, but what really took me by surprise was what happened next.

"Welcome," the other face of stone spoke. "Welcome. You are here."

"Yes," said Anisie. "The Messenger is with us, and a new one, another companion on this Journey – Cara, her Guardian. Beautiful spirits with compassion and adventure are always needed."

"Yes, dear one," the voice bellowed. "Yes. These times – those times – are upon us. Things are changing, and not for the better. There are forces in motion, and –"

"I hear you. We are at your service." Anisie nodded, and for some reason, so did I. Somehow, I wasn't afraid, though I knew there would indeed be dangerous times ahead.

The clouds started to roll in. The sky went from a pristine blue to a dark, menacing grey. The wind picked up and started to become a gale. The hairs on my neck started to stand on end.

They started...

"It is time, young ones, to learn, to experience. It is time to go on the paths of olde, to follow the paths of the new. It is time to experience; it is time to understand. For this is all part of Our Story, and Yours." Both faces of stone spoke harmoniously, but the tones of their voices were like the deep tones of bells you hear from church towers. Harriet and I both nodded at the same time instinctively, both feeling a sense of excitement and wonder. Then, it went black. Then, there was Light. Then there were Stars. An expanse. The Milky Way. Then, there was Andromeda, our neighbouring galaxy. I remembered my studies of astronomy. Then there was a swirl of blue dust which became a door, and what we saw was something I had never seen in my lifetime.

We walked through and saw a high drystone wall. There were cats, but not quite cats – they were beings that walked on two legs – and women in armour that walked like clockwork, whose faces were human but not, their expressions fixed and unwavering. There was a huge clock in the sky with pointed hands and a background of black latticework on the clock face. It was like Big Ben, but there were also pyramids in the background, and not far away was the Sphinx... A cat, well, a cat-like being, looked at me.

"Welcome," she said. "Welcome to Bubastis: The City Of Cats." She smiled. How did I know she was female? "Anything is possible here," she said, as if she could read my mind. "And gifts, whatever you have, they are amplified." I nodded.

The three of us walked up into a pyramid surrounded by statues of cats. We walked up what seemed to be an endless staircase. At the top was a door of magenta, and when we got inside, three beautiful women of colour, skin emanating a dark brown like chocolate, greeted us. "Welcome," they said in unison, "Welcome to the City Of Bubastis."

I had to look twice. I thought I saw the women change into cats and then change back. They smiled at me. All three. "Trust your senses, your gut instinct, not your eyes. What is possible... There are things that make sense, but don't, and things that don't, but do. You must trust your Path."

"Yes," said another voice. I gasped. So many things I had been reading about. I looked at her, but somehow, I knew – it was Hypatia, one of the first women mathematicians and astronomers from Egypt.

My mind began to sing with so much Possibility. "Yes," another voice joined in. It was Queen Amanirenas who had fought against the Romans.

"Yes," said another voice. It was Queen Odae, one of the Aziza, and leader of the Faeries from the planet Ariendes. Selena had told me about her when we first met at the Snow Queene's castle.

The three women all joined in unison. "Welcome to our realm, the city within a city, a dream within a dream. Welcome to Bubastis." All of us smiled. We knew that our lives would never be the same. Let the adventure begin.

Chapter Fifteen:
Harriet Is On Another Journey

WE stayed a few nights in this beautiful, unique place with so much mystery and so many secrets – I knew I wouldn't be able to unravel them all. I, Harriet, was writing a novel that I didn't know if anyone would read – would it see the light of day? I was doing it anyway. Hopefully, it would make enough to get my son out of there, out of that place – the Farm – before it was too late. But I knew that being at Bubastis, I would learn so much more. It might not fit in with my book, but I knew that it would lift my spirit and help me to continue. Not just with writing the book, but with living this life, taking one step at a time, placing one foot in front of the other. That's what I have always known, even before I got to the lair of the Snow Queene.

There's so much to learn, I thought, and the woman draped in red silk, Queen Amanirenas, agreed, as if reading my mind.

Over a breakfast of porridge, she said, "Yes, there is so much to learn, but you will have time. Don't make haste. Take in the surroundings. You will learn what you need to – in time. Be Patient." I nodded, feeling relieved, and the Queen must have sensed that, as she said, "Just take it in,

Harriet. Take it in, and everything will fall into place. The course has been set. It is now up to you to take the first step. That is all."

I nodded again and then tucked into my porridge. I knew I would need a lot of sustenance for The Journey ahead. Suddenly, I had a vision: An Angel's wisp... wings... We were walking towards the Sun, sand... the Eye Of... We didn't know, but I had a feeling. Queen Amanirenas just smiled, as if she knew what I was experiencing. This Queen was surrounded not only by her Ancestors, but by other Mystical forces – things that I would never understand. The Queen looked at me with her brown eyes twinkling. She knew what I had just realized, and I was okay to not know more – for the moment. But one day, I hope to learn more about this woman, this place, and my connection to it all.

After breakfast, soon after the first Light, we were off, making our way to the desert. I thought we would have needed clothes, loose-fitting cotton clothes and head cloths to shield us from the sun, wind, and sand, but just before breakfast, one of the cats that morphed into a woman from time to time had said that we didn't – we could dress as we liked. I was surprised. I walked to the breakfast room, a beautiful chamber inundated with the colour of sapphire, to eat. When we entered what was known as the Sun room after breakfast – a large chamber bathed in sunlight from dusk until dawn – I got an inkling about the next Journey. I had a feeling.

We all stood in the centre of the chamber in a circle, and we were instructed to hold hands and close our eyes. When we opened them, we were surrounded by an orb of deep lavender light. I gasped in surprise at the many things I was seeing. Me, I was a woman who worked so hard and was treated so horribly by what was considered a foster family, and yet, now, I was seeing what was actually Possible – if only I could tell my boy! But this adventure was necessary for me to know who I am. It might fuel the writing for my book, and if not, it would fuel my spirit and my son's. And who knows, maybe I would write about it in another book – you can never tell.

I continued to be awash in wonder, gazing at the bubble of deep lavender. I closed my eyes again, just experiencing and enjoying the adventure, enjoying the experience of being in the moment. I was learning, and at that realization, a small smile crossed my face. When I opened my eyes again, we appeared in the desert, still surrounded by the bubble of deep lavender. Cara, Oceantis, Staerkie, and I suddenly faced golden dunes of sand. I realized we were in the Sahara. I couldn't believe it. As soon as we touched the golden mounds of sand, still in the bubble, we saw a woman in the distance. A tall woman with two ravens, one on each shoulder. There was also a woman, a tall young woman – a bit shorter – with her, who had jet black hair, and you could tell there was a connection. Somehow, their lives intersected. I couldn't quite figure it out, but there was something there. And me – I was a part of it somehow, but I still didn't know how. It was all clouds and mist, mist and fog. But that will all disappear, and I knew when that happened, I would see a lot more clearly.

The woman with the two ravens said, "Come with us," so we did. The bubble of lavender surrounded all of us, including the two women we had just met, and we started rising and rising, going faster into the air, almost surging into the sky. I had to close my eyes as I was a little afraid of heights and felt I had to brace myself, even though I knew I would be safe. I then opened my eyes; we were in the air, the sky, an ocean of teal. We saw the sun setting, an orb of fiery orange and gold. I smiled and looked around at all of us, including Cara, Oceantis, and Staerkie. We all had the same expression – Mother Nature was Beauty. The woman with the two ravens then spoke. "Look down." So we did.

We all gasped. Below us, in her finery, was a circle – a concentric shape of blue, a light cerulean, swirls of it, like a whirlpool of colour. There were also shades of a golden brown, and I even saw some shades of aubergine. The circle glimmered in the rays of the setting sun. We started to float… Down, Down, Down… I started to take a deep breath. Staerkie touched my shoulder – I looked at her, and she looked back at me reassuringly. I continued to just focus on the setting sun, her rays, and then I looked down again. Somehow, I felt a lot better. We continued to come down, and then the light disappeared. It became black, and then it was dotted with stars. We were still Falling, Falling, Descending – we all saw stars, comets, and many nebulae – the magical star factories. Then, a book appeared in this maelstrom of Light, then a sword, then an hourglass. The hourglass started to turn, turn, turn – around and around, faster and faster – like it was a spinning image of Light and Sound creating a whirlpool of aquamarine, magenta, amethyst, and gold. All our bodies became engulfed in the maelstrom, this frenetic symphony of Light and sound. The Symphony of Light and Sound, a music that entranced me. I, Harriet, was taken aback by what I had seen so far. I closed my eyes, and then…

When I opened them again, I gasped – we were all surrounded, engulfed, in water. Carriages from the 17th and

18th centuries appeared, but they had fins like whales or dolphins. As I looked closer, I noticed that these carriages were automatons, but they were not rusting, just emitting a silver glow. And there were lions – yes, lions – but they had fins and tails like mermaids… Mer-lions? I didn't know such a thing existed, but there they were – mer-lions, mer-men, and angels that also flew through water. I also saw people who were also automatons, glowing a similar silver aura, and despite being many leagues under water, had no hint of rust. I then looked at the woman who now had doves on her shoulders, and suddenly they turned into eagles. I figured out that the ravens must be shape-shifters. The woman, called Magda, now looked at me, nodded, and then disappeared.

Below us, there was a moat, and we floated above it, right into the castle's depths. We walked up the stairs and saw another Mer-lion with a crown on his head, standing next to his Queen, the Queen Mer-lion or lioness. They spoke in a language that none of us understood until they said, "Welcome to Atlantis." I gasped, but I knew the wonders had just Begun.

"Why are we here?" asked Cara, my Guardian and Protector.

"You will see, in time," said the Mer-lion. "There are many secrets and mysteries in our lair – so many… And we are connected to other worlds, such as Tír na nÓg, the land of the ones who never age and never die. Yes, Yes. But this is our story, ours to tell you… the genesis of Atlantis."

All of us listened, and this was their tale…

Chapter Sixteen:
The Mer-lions Of Atlantis

MERAIN, the Mer-lion of Atlantis, had five sets of twins – four sets were boys; however, the youngest pair were girls, mer-lionesses. Each child was a leader of a kingdom, a role they fulfilled from birth. The twin mer-lionesses were shape-shifters, as were all the mer-lions. They could be human, fish, faerie – whatever they chose. They were also related to the mystical beings of Tír na nÓg. The mer-lionesses were unique, however, as they were born from the stars up above. The goddesses of the stars, who watched over all universes, also created a sea of starlight, twilight, and stardust. The universe up above mirrored the one in the watery depths below in Atlantis. In the celestial realm, they also had five sets of twins watch over their kingdom. One star goddess, who was also a cousin of a faerie in Tír na nÓg, had a daughter; the father was unknown, but the daughter was said to be a Keeper Of the Sea Lions of Neptune. She was Navaen, the star goddess's daughter, who could shape-shift into black holes, shooting stars, and so on. She, along with the Sea Lions of Neptune, also watched over the Nebulae, the star-making factories of the heavens.

The Sea Lions of Neptune were also relatives of the Mer-lions of Atlantis. The Sea Lions Of Neptune, The Saekandes, were a part of that Mystical Force… When the twin girls, the Mer-Lionesses were born, the Sea Lions Of Neptune all pledged to keep them safe, and each family from the Cosmos decided to give them gifts. One was a poetess from Neptune. She gave them the gift of music and song. Another was a librarian. She was from the star region not far from Saturn. She gave them the gift of knowledge and critical thought. Another was a famous warrior who came from Mars. She was a faerie knowledgeable in swordsmanship, martial arts, and the ways of the sea – she originally came from Atlantis but decided to go to Mars to carve out a life separate from the kingdom in Atlantis. She loved the mer-family but had to be her own independent spirit to carve out her life in a different world.

When the twin mer-lionesses were growing up, they went on several magical journeys. One was the defense of a celestial realm known for bright shooting stars. These twinkling orbs helped travelers pass through black holes to different worlds – they were cousins of Stargette, the bright and engaging guide to Anisie, the Spider Queen, and Selena. One black hole had unicorns who were the guardians of these portals to different worlds. Some worlds were benevolent, and some were not, but the unicorns made sure that these evil spirits did not leave those black holes. However, one day, the unicorns disappeared, and evil ghosts or spirits escaped from the black holes, intent on destroying the universe that the unicorns had wanted to defend. It was said that the trouble had started on Mars, the Red Planet.

The twin mer-girls caught wind of this. They longed for adventure, as they were only fifteen; however, their culture had determined that girls were to be raised in the ways of traditional femininity, sewing with threads from the silk of Lady Vertania, the moon, and creating tunics for the men, the mer-lions, and blue cloaks that would ward off evil. The girls were at their looms in their castle in Atlantis when they heard that something was afoot. They cast aside their threads and looms, put on their armour, and shape-shifted into human beings. They could only do this when the moon was full, when Lady Vertania was at her brightest, for three days. When the moon, Lady Vertania, would begin to wane, Sasha and Sentina had to be mer-lions once again.

The two set off, Sasha and Sentina, for Mars, their chain mail and swords at the ready. Their armour was made from a silver only found in Atlantis, their chain mail and swords made from a metal only found in the lair of Lady Vertania. As young human women, they closed their eyes and flew: Flew, Flew, FLEW into the OtherWorld – Mars. Red was everywhere – Red in the sky, Red on the earth. They looked around. There they were – an Army Of Beasts. The Mocturna. Sometimes they were part man, part Beast – they had descended from a man who had been bitten by a wolf that was bitten by a vampire. Their eyes were savage and red, like the planet they were on. They stumbled along on two human legs, but the rest of their bodies were animal-like, covered with jet black fur. Their wolf-like faces had hauntingly red, beady eyes. Other times, they could totally transform into a wolf form.

The two girls closed their eyes. Bubbles of silver surrounded them – silver forged by elves, as well as by Magda, one of the Sister Warriors of the Tuatha Dé Danann, for Magda had several gifts. With the help of Magda and several druids that appeared armed with daggers, the twin mer-sisters were ready for battle. They then closed their eyes and flew into the air, which was easier to do in their human form. With their imagination, they incorporated the movements of tigers, dragons, and eagles, amassing great speed, agility, and physical prowess. Sasha and Sentina soared up into the sky to incredible heights, blocking with their hands and feet, then slinking in the air like snakes, before crouching and pouncing like tigers. They remembered their Master who taught them various martial arts: karate, kung fu, and jujitsu. They were all based on one thing: observation of the natural world. And this Master, their guide to the world of martial arts, would take them to the Serengeti, to Asia, and around the world to observe Mother Nature In Action. The two mer-sisters flipped, doing an aerial ballet, going in circles, flitting about from left to right, and traversing space and time. They did. Yes. Yes.

"Sasha," screamed Sentina, "Watch out!" Sasha almost got hit by a huge ball of deep scarlet light that shot out of one of the Mocturna's eyes. The Sisters shivered. They shivered. Another Mocturna shape-shifted fully into a human man, did some flips and somersaults, and threw some daggers that circled into the air, increasing in speed, and almost hit Sasha… But with one karate move, one of the druids kicked the daggers away from Sasha. Yes, it had just begun. Sasha echoed her sister's bravery and did some flips, hurling her body into the air. She became a flame of Fire and, with one breath, her flames began hitting the army of Mocturna like dominoes. There were explosions, and many bodies burst apart in flames, One after another – boom, boom, Boom!

Then, a woman made entirely out of silver appeared –

the silver from the realm of Lady Vertania. She was a Dark Angel of Silver Light. The woman closed her eyes, and sparks of ice from Lady Vertania's frozen depths darted from the woman's direction. Sentina avoided them, but Sasha was hit.

"Sister!" Sentina screamed. She added, "BE Careful." Blood was everywhere, a crimson rain. Sasha had started to descend quite quickly to the ground of Mars. She was about to hit the ground when another Mer-lioness had appeared. She manifested into a human woman with robes of silver, and hieroglyphics appeared on her azure robes. She brandished a sword and closed her eyes. In seconds, she did a series of backflips, front flips, and circling movements that suddenly became a glowing ball of anger and aggression. This human ball spun faster and faster until she became a ray of Light, aquamarine and emerald Light which shot out at the entire army of Mocturna. There was an even bigger explosion – a tsunami of light, a storm of crescendos, screams, and cries. Then there was Silence. There was nothing. It was like the war had never existed. The woman in azure robes looked at the two girls; she shook her head and sighed. The woman put her hand out to Sasha, and instantly her wounds were healed. Her twin sister, Sentina, hugged her, and they both flew toward the woman. It was their mother, Verina. She was the Queen Mer-lioness of Atlantis. She had ascended from the depths of her watery Kingdom to the celestial Kingdom of the stars ruled by the Sea Lions Of Neptune.

"It is time to come home, my girls." They both nodded. The three embraced each other and disappeared, suddenly reappearing in Atlantis. The unicorns suddenly reappeared in front of the gateways, the portals of the black holes, as the star goddesses were now free from their prisons as soon as the Mocturna were killed. Balance was back in the universe, and the unicorns would prevent any evil entities from escaping through the black holes. Verina had decided that her two twin girls would be trained as warriors and intellectuals, having learned that letting someone's gender determine their destiny was not right. Their destiny should be decided by that person's heart and spirit instead.

The King of Atlantis looked at all of us, smiling from his throne. "This is part of our story, and those girls, the twin girls, are now rulers of Aquiriantis, a Kingdom that is part of Atlantis," said Seragaen, the King, quietly but proudly. "For Atlantis," he continued, "has ten kingdoms in total. Those two Queen Mer-lionesses are my Aunts – warriors and intellectuals. He looked at the tall woman with magenta hair and the one with hair of shining teal, as well as the rest of us, and said, "You are all welcome to rest."

He looked closer at me. "You," he said quietly. "You are on another journey, and there is one who will guide you. Go through that door – the green one – with all the others… She will appear to you. She will appear to you, for she has a Story to tell – a Story that involves you." I nodded, excited, but I had a lump in my throat. I indeed went through that door with the other women and knew that more revelations would await me.

A mer-woman, who suddenly shapeshifted into a mer-lioness, walked us to a beautiful pyramid of silver. Entering, we soon came upon a chamber, a chamber filled with books, all glittering underneath the water. But somehow, we could all breathe without any apparatus.

"You must know what is Possible, Harriet," said the mer-lioness. A book, the colour of emeralds, suddenly floated into her hands. "You must –" she smiled. "You must read about your lineage." She smiled again and then disappeared.

I looked down, and the book suddenly appeared in my hands. I, a young woman, a young black woman, treated so horribly by the family who took me in – I, Harriet E. Wilson, could not believe my eyes. The others who were with me were also astounded and took books from the shelves – these also were not damaged even though they were submerged under water. Crescendos of teal upon teal, azure upon azure. It was a hallowed space, this library, filled with magic and wonder – this room submerged in The Aquatic World. There were also books that spun around like in a liquid maelstrom, including one book that echoed memories – one book that echoed mirrors, reflections, and manifestations of worlds recreated…

In my mind's eye, the word Worcester came up, and I then saw a man with a short white beard, flowing light brown robes, and piercing brown eyes… The name Edward Talbot came up, and the word again – Worcester… I knew that these words would matter in time. Other words came up: Fenian… St. Patrick… I also saw a light brown map, and other colours rushed into my mind, filling me to the core. I saw a group of people in bright clothing… scarlet, amaranthine, gold, and saffron – with golden horned helmets on their heads. And there were other symbols, indicative of a way of being – a celestial, otherworldly sense of the world… Who were they? What were they? These questions kept spinning around in my mind… But in the meantime,

I felt – I knew – from the gut, that I would know and be part of these worlds at another time. But now, I must keep the focus and the shift towards something I must know now.

"Yes," said the mer-lioness, "use, shift, your focus. Your attention must be on this so you may know your origins, discover your genesis, and hear the music of who you are – a synergy, a harmony, of all that you are."

I nodded, as if, somehow, I just knew. And so, I took the book, ready for another submersion, immersion into a world I did not know, but somehow knew – another world I was entering, a trip into the fantastic, a realm filled with Possibility and The Dreaming. I looked again at the books swirling around in the water and the ones on the bookshelves – amazingly, they were all intact, not damaged at all – it was as if being surrounded by liquid didn't matter.

My companions all sat down on cushions that appeared out of nowhere, and I sat down on a magenta one decorated with sea horses, mermaids, sirens, and a mystical being that looked like the mer-lioness that we were just talking to. I opened this gorgeous book that was gilded with gold. At this, I heard a sound like chiming bells, then the sound of seashells, like conch shells being used as a xylophone, being touched softly with a wooden-headed hammer such as one made from rosewood; how I knew this, I just didn't know, but I did. The pages seemed to speak to me, and so the Story Began.

Chapter Seventeen:
Psoraes

FLASHES Of Light. Wings of a dove... Beautiful women, radiating lavender and darker shades of violet... So many things were converging all at the same time – ripples, there are so many ripples. Since 2000 B.C., it was found that a certain plant along the Nile stopped this flaking, patchiness, and redness of the skin. Activated, sparked by the Light. They knew of her power: it was the Psoraes. They Knew; They Remembered. The Psoraes are the purple ones, known for healing, known for Sparking The Spirit. He smiled. Baniti lived in the village near the Nile, and he knew of them, knew that the Psoraes had many secrets, including that Mother Nature was a Healer, if you paid attention. If you paid attention and saw her Bounty. The Psoraes, mystical beings with wings of bright violet, sang songs of Mother Nature's Healing Magic, and Baniti wanted to not only tell that Story but bring about healing, not just of the body, but of the mind. The Psoraes knew about this balance, the equation – the relationship – between mind, body, and spirit. They had known since before Time began. The Psoraes were angels, musical beings from on high.

One day, as Baniti was thinking deeply while sitting along the banks of the River Nile, a bright presence of mauve and gold came to him and whispered, "Come with me." Baniti opened his eyes, and they were at the top of the Himalayas. He gasped. The woman of mauve and gold just looked at him and smiled as she hovered in the air, her bright mauve wings lit up by the golden sun. The woman started to tell him. "My people, we are known for being healers, restoring the balance. For example, there are times we must be at Rest and other times when our bodies must be engaged in activity. Too much of one or the other can create illness, disease. We – my sister, Kaya, and I – wanted to create a community, a fellowship, where those in need can be healed. A place of sanctuary, a place of peace and meditation, but also a place of joy and creativity." Baniti nodded, as he had the same dream.

Before you know it, a village came to be: one that used hieroglyphics, but also the symbols of the Adinkra. Buildings were made out of sand, stone, mud, and water. Yes. The sisters from the Psoraes welcomed into the village those whose hair had been prematurely grey from hard labour, from working long days in fields around the Nile, especially when she was fertile from the annual floods. Yes, the ones with skin, hardened like leather, those who had walked through the Desert, going to different worlds. The Psoraes closed their eyes, and from their fingertips appeared an ointment, an elixir that made people's faces like new – their wrinkles disappeared. Those toiling in the earth found relief; they had experienced a calm – even a joy – they had not felt in years. Poetry was read and tales were spun. The Power Of Story gave hope to those in this village, this sanctuary not far from the Nile. Baniti was pleased he could help these people; the yellowish-brown powder from the plants he found along the river also helped the skin. There was joy, peace, and a Celebration of Life at this sanctuary with the two Psoraes sisters at the helm and the guidance of Baniti – The coming together between Immortal and Mortal. The sun goddess, Isis, smiled; it was a Beautiful sight to behold.

Having read this story, my mind was now back in Atlantis, part of the world that was a part of the realm of Poseidon, the Eye Of Africa that was formed by a meteorite that struck the realm of ice in what was later known as Groenland, melting parts of it, and causing a flood that submerged whole areas into an aquatic darkness, until new civilizations came forth, like Atlantis.

I remembered what was said to me by the Cyaen. They knew about the mystery that was the Eye of Africa and Her Power. The Cyaen, faeries enrobed in dark indigo or greenish blue, watched over the Sahara and all people that crossed this Desert. After thinking about this remarkable, mystical circle of women, I closed the book of emerald. I had never thought I would see these things – Atlantis, the Eye of Africa, or to start this Odyssey. A mystical bunch of seeds that have been dug into the soil, seeds that have started to germinate. I am seeing into the Egyptian culture. I have also met Queen Amanirenas, the unforgettable queen of the Kush Empire, next door to neighbouring Egypt. Tears rushed to my eyes. Now, they streamed down my cheeks. It was my time. I never thought I would see Africa, let alone Egypt, or the Eye of Africa. That part of myself was being heard, and I was coming more into balance. Seeing Queen Amanirenas, the one-eyed Queen – my father would often say that we had Egyptian roots, but we were also a part of the Ashanti tribe, and those Ancestors were the Akan people. Their symbolic language was the Adinkra.

I remembered the sanctuary created by Baniti and the Psoraes in the story I had just read, The Ones With Wings of Vibrant Lavender and Violet. But there was more to come. The Irish part of myself was calling; I was hearing voices, singing – so much singing – and the Celtic beat, the Celtic drums. And I saw my Irish mother with skin the colour of alabaster, her eyes a blazing brown, a fiery chestnut brown with shades of hazel. Her name, Margaret, rang in my mind like the chiming of bells. Then, I saw people with hooded faces walking around a tree, an oak tree, covered with so many branches and leaves of green, and with so many roots underground. The people, they were walking in robes of red. Then, there was a woman dressed in leather, brandishing a sword; I was remembering, and the currents were breaking forth like a chiming of sound, of sea, of aquatic echoes, bursting through time and space. My mother would sing to me:

> My Bonnie lies over the ocean,
> My Bonnie lies over the sea,
> My Bonnie lies over the ocean,
> So, bring back my Bonnie to me.

I Remembered, and I was Remembering – crescendos of Light and Sound, lightning flashing, thunder, bursts of clouds dripping in black ink; I was remembering the currents of the drumbeat, the Celtic drums were sounding, my Mother's voice… then, I saw a woman with ravens, one on each shoulder, they were cawing, cawing, and then in a flash, the birds became white, now doves. The woman's hair a jetblack, a ravenous jetblack, and her eyes flashing silver, violet, a shining cobalt, then, a fiery, unforgettable gold. She said, "My name is Magda. I am part of the Tuatha Dé Danann. I am a Spark, An Ember, and so is your mother. And so are you – you are a part of it. You were always a part of it – no matter what people tell you, you are a part of it, and so you must not forget. Do not forget – you are a part of –"

I opened my eyes, looked at this beautiful book of emerald, and was met with Silence. I then felt the same choral music, a music of echoing bells, a tinkling of Beauty. I picked up the book again and turned to the next chapter.

144

Chapter Eighteen:
Mysticus

FAERIE Bells – the Stargaenes were singing... The Carillion Music Faeries, whose language was song that reverberated throughout the universe in times of good and bad... The Stargaenes listened with anticipation as the river waters glimmered in response along the North Saskatchewan. The mystical creatures played and danced among the bells that were no longer in existence in the mortal world, but in theirs, they still existed. They played on their harps, clinked cups of silver together, and shook bracelets made with rubies and emeralds. The faeries, the scholars, perusing their tomes, sat back for a bit and listened, and the ones guarding the museum – echoing one in New York City that held dear The Starry Night by the famed redheaded one and other masterpieces – they also stood back and listened.

Madame Soleil smiled and smiled with joy as her rays reached out to all who needed her, especially after the forest fires that enshrouded the City North of the 49th parallel in smoke, a veil that blocked out Madame Soleil for weeks as people with asthma and other respiratory issues had to take cover and stay home whenever possible.

The Festival Of Festivals proclaimed Theatre as the

Mainstay, as the Inspiration heralding The City Within The City, with landmarks like the Armoury that had her own story. Yes, Yes, the place that was the place of Old – a place of memories and dreams. Sometimes, one of dashed hopes – a place where a woman was betrothed but her beloved left her at the altar, and she hung herself, her body in a white wedding dress, a figure of virginal white hanging like a hauntingly macabre chandelier.

Yes, Memories never sleep in this place, and the Library, the haven for all, had more Stories. The City Within The City that never slept. The City Within The City that had a character unmatched by others. A City Within The City, where angels roamed, ghosts lurked, and Magic was The Currency Of Dreams. Vision. Gold wings. She appeared on the water: Obourous... Obourous... Obourous...

And then there were others, Dancing In The Sunset... The Dusk beckons them. Auroralae, The Beings Of Light; Synergy. Stargine remembered them – some were her Sisters. I smiled, as I had met Stargine's other sister, Stargette. Stargette was a very young star, but to us, she would be Ancient, being a couple of millennia years old. I smiled, happy to have met this mystical and youthful spirit that was a faithful, loyal, and protective companion to Selena and Anisie, the Spider Queen. I then continued to read the next page. And So They Lurked, the Auroralae – they Sparked and Jumped, Joyous with Beams Of Golden Light, especially in places that needed love and hope. Stargine saw these curious human beings from her lookout point, perched on the banks of the North Saskatchewan, not far from The City Within The City, Old Strathcona.

Venus. Orbit. Shooting Stars. They manifested in the Universe into Starlings, Celestial Beings of Light, Celestial

Light Forces like Stargine. They danced and played, danced and played, until one day, one of their faerie princesses disappeared.

"What do we do?" they cried. "She is precious, so Precious to us, as she is one of the few with a heart made out of Kurulean crystal, as she always looked out for others." Three starlings came forth – Stargine's sisters: Regulaes, Furgene, and Cendraella. They were from the Constellation Orion.

"We'll find her," they exclaimed. "We will find her." From near and far they searched, looking under meteorites, shooting stars, looking into Black Holes, until they found a clue: shimmering Star Dust in the form of a harp. "She loved music, our Princess... She loved –" The Three Sisters Of Light sighed. They kept flying forward, sometimes stopping to walk on rays of Light and the pathways of other stars. Then, they came to a golden telescope. In front of it was Kurdane, an astronomer to all that was in The Universe.

"What are you looking for, my girls? What do you seek?"

"We seek the presence of our Dear Princess. Do you know where she is?"

Kurdane thought for a moment. "Wait – I heard something, some chatter among some of the Star goddesses. There is One who wanted to seek the Power of a Starling and would stop at nothing. They also said he tried once before but was denied. As punishment and revenge, he trapped a starling in a stained-glass window in the realm of Gaea. The family of the starling was devastated. The starling has not been seen since. As for the princess, they say that they are connected, as the starling and the princess are cousins. I'd say if you find the starling, the princess might not be far behind."

The Trio of Light looked at each other. They then shook their heads. "What do we do?" Then, they saw a flash of Light. Then another. And another. Emerald, azure, vermillion, and gold – shimmering lights of various, vibrant colours. They looked for The Source. It was from the planet of the seven seas in the realm of Gaea. They shot like shooting stars down below to the planet called Earth. They were flying as if faster than the speed of Light, as they were mystical beings of The Universe and sisters to Stargine. They saw golden sheets of Light emanating even more of a golden glow. They flew north of the 49th parallel to the Land named after one of Queen Victoria's daughters.

They Flew, Flew, and saw footprints of golden Light on the River called The North Saskatchewan. They continued to Fly until they saw a golden-brown building made out of sandstone and granite. They descended through the dome that had palm trees in the highest gallery. They continued to descend until they saw a woman featured in stained glass, wearing a toga and carrying a sheaf of wheat. They looked into her eyes, the depiction of this woman. Her eyes were blue, but the princess's eyes were a deep, unforgettable violet. The hair was blonde, but the princess they were looking for had hair that was a raven black. They looked closer, peering at the image being depicted. At the side of the woman, they saw beautiful red roses. It was a wild rose, one of the princess's favourite flowers. Surrounding the image of the woman were colours such as a shimmering emerald, azure, gold, and so on. Being a princess of the Starlings, Verconia was assigned Guardian Lights from birth to protect her. Suddenly, the colours started to glow. They started to take shape – the colours were people, the People of the Light, the Guardians of the Starlings. Men, women, people in their uniforms – they all nodded, then saluted. The woman featured in the stained-glass window also started to transform – deep violet eyes appeared, and jet-black hair, the colour of night. It was the Princess! Her toga changed into a dress of the most unforgettable hue of blue – A bright, bold cerulean.

"Princess, we have found you at long last," exclaimed the three Sisters Of Light. "We have been looking for you everywhere." The princess smiled, and one of the wild roses in the painting of glass started to move and shake. There was a burst of Light – it was a starling, the one that many were previously looking for, including Stargine.

"I'm free at last," she sighed. "I had almost lost hope."

"We are here now," said one of the Illuminated Ones. "We will take you all home."

Both the Princess and the Starling nodded, flying with the Trio from Gaea to their world. There was a big celebration, and a myriad of shooting stars marked the occasion with Bursts Of Light And Sound.

150

Chapter Nineteen:
The Mocturna: The Werewolves Of Lady Vertania

I smiled as I turned the page. The beautiful choral music of bells and now, angelic voices joined together to create an ethereal harmony. It encouraged me to continue, to read more of these tales that were lifting me up, and I heard my mother's voice in my head. It made me happy, and I experienced waves of joy.

On the next ivory page of the book, there was a dragon with seven heads and seven crowns of gold in battle with a woman surrounded by the Sun, with Lady Vertania, the Moon, beside her, and her aura shining down on her feet – the battle was shrouded with darkness. But there were also creatures with four legs that descended onto the earth and were destined to roam Gaia for all time. These were the Mocturna, the werewolves of Lady Vertania. They manifested when the breath of the dragon intermingled with the silvery ground and celestial waters of Lady Vertania. Her depths and their life force circulated in the otherworldly lunar sanctum and formed their bodies, their fur, their bright red tongues, and unforgettable fiery gold eyes. They were known as the Curandaes. Their other genesis, the second bloodline, the Verjandaes, came from a human who was bitten by a wolf that was bitten by a vampire.

The two groups never got along, and there was a millennia-long feud that seemed to get more mired in hatred and resentment as Time went on. Both were the guardians of the moon, the Lady Vertania – one group watched over one side of the moon, the other group kept guard over the other. Both tribes of The Mocturna walked around, keeping watch over the craters, hills, valleys, and mountains on the surface of the realm that is Lady Vertania, the moon.

All of the Mocturna, these werewolves, were shape-shifters. They could take human form and fly down to Earth to be among the human beings who made Earth home. And one of these wolves, one of these Mocturna, became lonely walking the earth. He decided to go to university and become a teacher – maybe then, he would find a way to not only impart knowledge but also find companionship on a planet surrounded by the stars, which reminded him of the other world. He studied hard, got his Bachelor's, Master's, and Doctorate, then started teaching. On the way, he fell in love with another teacher, a professor from the college. They would take romantic walks in a park filled with green: oak trees and also yew trees, portals to different worlds, and laughed. The two started to get to know each other better. And one night, they walked towards a Yew tree, all alone, holding hands. They got close, and the tree opened up. A portal appeared, which got larger and larger – they walked closer, curious, and then got sucked inside. Inside, there were stars, so many stars.

"Where are we?" asked the woman, the fellow professor. "Where are we going?"

"I don't know," said Stephen, a Mocturna, "I just don't know." He shouted, "Hold on to me!"

They spun around and around, the bodies hurtling through space, surrounded by sounds, screams even. They were then standing on the ground. They looked up. They saw the body of a young man standing against a tree. A huge raven was on his neck. They didn't know what to do. Stephen and Gwen looked to the left. They looked. They wondered. Suddenly, Stephen changed into his wolf form, the Mocturna of Lady Vertania. His woman friend, Gwen, changed into a unicorn. They both saw a chariot. Magda, one of the Tuatha Dé Danann, who often had as her companions two ravens, one on each shoulder, appeared in the mist. Magda did not want this young man, his body propped up against a tree, to die, as she had a vision. She looked at the body and screamed – screamed, and cried, her tears drowning her creamy ivory skin. For she had a vision that he would fight his best friend, but later on, there would be another battle to the death, and he would cross the threshold into the other world – the world of those who had left the mortal lair, The Dead.

Some men approached. They had been chasing the young man, particularly one of them, Lugaid mac Con Roí – as this young man had slept with Lugaid's mother, so he wanted revenge. They hunted him down. He was outnumbered, and they had cut out his entrails. He asked to walk to a nearby lake to get some water to drink, his last request. He sought a pause… and then, they came to finish him off.

Stephen tried to ward them off, but to no avail – there were too many. Stephen was somehow hurled into the air, and the men came closer. They thought at first that this warrior, Cúchulainn, was dead, but they were not sure. Looking again, the men found that he was indeed dead.

They chopped off his head, but then, something unexpected happened – the sword from his lifeless hand fell on the arm of Lugaid mac Con Roí and chopped it off.

Then, when news spread of Cúchulainn's death, his good friend and fellow warrior, Conall Cernach, who had vowed to defend his honour, came in vengeance to battle this man who felled Cúchulainn. Stephen suddenly saw it from outside, as did Gwen – it was like peering into a Looking Glass. Stephen and Gwen could only see what was happening, but they could no longer help.

The two fought valiantly, with Conall binding one arm behind his back, as requested by the one-armed Lugaid. Conall and Lugaid continued fighting with swords, the battle at equal strength until, with Conall's signal, his horse took one big bite out of Lugaid's side. Lugaid was in shock as he watched his entrails spill onto the ground.

"That wasn't fair," he cried. "An unfair advantage."

But Conall replied, "I had already put my arm behind my back as you had only one arm, but nothing was said about animals." Lugaid remembered the agreement made before battle – the surprise was still frozen on his face as his head was chopped off by Conall. Stephen nodded, as did Conall, feeling at peace for avenging his friend and fellow warrior. Stephen saw Gwen, his woman friend, still a unicorn, and nodded again.

A faerie appeared from Tír na nÓg and nodded. There was a twinkle in her eye. Suddenly, the two, Stephen and Gwen, appeared in front of a shop. It was in Greenwich, London, home of the meridian timeline from which time was created. Sparked by the impending seriousness of a devastatingly large number of ships colliding on the ocean due to the lack of reliable navigation, the creation of longitude based on the meridian timeline in Greenwich and a reliable marine chronometer by John Harrison, the H4, prevented many deaths. A pocket watch inspired by the H4 was in a glass display case along with a thumb ring. It shone red like a rowan berry. Gwen was captured, enthralled by it. Stephen bought it for her and got the old-fashioned pocket watch for himself. They left the store and walked around that part of London. They entered the gates that led to the old Naval College, which used to be the Greenwich Hospital, which housed retired sailors, the dream of Queen Mary II made manifest by King William III. They walked around.

There was a fence, a black, wrought iron fence right across from the Queen's House, where Queen Henrietta Maria, wife of Charles I, lived. The house was now a naval museum. On the black wrought iron fence was a symbol — a mer-lion with two golden tridents, one on each side.

Stephen closed his eyes; he didn't know why, but he did. Gwen did the same thing. Suddenly, they were surrounded by clouds of light and sound, and there was a jerk. They opened their eyes, and Stephen was bathing in a river, and Gwen was a princess dressed in robes of velvet, but she was on the shore. Gwen had the thumb ring on her finger. At that moment, a monster, a serpent, rose out of the water. It was about to devour Stephen when Gwen quickly saw what was happening — a spear suddenly appeared in her hand. She threw it to Stephen, and he quickly killed the serpent. Falling in love with the quick-thinking princess, Stephen came out of the water, held her hand, and the thumb ring started to be engulfed in a lavender glow.

The King, who was in his quarters playing chess, saw the lavender glow in his mirror and telepathically summoned the Princess. "Arigaen, what has happened?"

"Father, there was a serpent, a sea serpent that suddenly appeared in the water, in the lake. There was a man bathing. I was on the shore not far away and saw the danger. I summoned a spear, threw it to him, and he killed the serpent. He loves me, Father, and wants my hand in marriage. What say you?"

"Daughter, not only are you beautiful, but you are also brave and compassionate. Yes, I give permission. Have him come to the castle."

Arigaen did, bringing her new love. The King asked for his dowry. The young lad remembered that his family had pigs, cows, oxen, and horses for a dowry. The King was pleased, and the two were married under the stars of the universe of the cosmos during Samhain – the time of the opening of different worlds… of different times… a new beginning. When the couple had begun their wedding night, Stephen and Gwen had woken up and were lying on the grassy hill before the Greenwich observatory. They could see London below, and the view was magnificent. They were on their own journey, but many others were within them: Dreams Within Dreams, Magic Within Magic.

Chapter Twenty:
Another Tale Of The Mocturna

THE rowan berry began to glow, bigger and bigger… Bigger and bigger… The Mocturna roamed on the moon, the surface of the realm of Lady Vertania, and another had descended on Earth. His name was Ronan, and he wanted to start a new life. He was tired of being stuck in a place where he couldn't determine his own destiny, as he was only meant to be a Guardian of Lady Vertania's realm. He was tired. He was ready for a change. He was walking around in London, went through Circuit Court, part of Floral Court, and onwards to Covent Garden. He went to the market there, but still he was lost – lost in purpose, lost in thought. Ronan then walked to the Temple Bar Memorial, which was quite some distance away, but he really wanted to be by himself, steeped in thought. He had so many decisions to make. What did he really want to do with his life? Where was he going? Where did he belong? Did he really want to stay on the path of being a Mocturna, or did he want to leave that life forever?

He couldn't undo the biology, but he didn't have to follow the code of being the guardian to Lady Vertania, the moon, as well as being required to help human beings when called for. He could just exist and lead some kind of life – solitary or maybe share it with someone – and just leave all the rest behind. That was an option. He could change at will – he was not forced to become the wolf whenever Lady Vertania shone bright in her full spherical self. He would think some more on what he had to do, and so when he saw the Black Dragon at the Temple Bar Memorial – not far from St. Paul's Cathedral – he suddenly felt at peace, like all the answers fell into place. Seeing this Mystical Beast put him at ease somehow. He knew that somehow he would find the answers, find out where he belonged, and when he did, there would be no doubt. That there was a place for him, even though he also came from a mystical line, just like this dragon. Yes, he knew that this dragon was a statue, but he also knew that there were many shape-shifters in London – this Londinium – and that this Dragon could be one of those, one of the Sisters that guards London, and especially Old London, harkening back to those days when she was the centre, and the Monarch had to meet the Lord Mayor at the gates to be given entry. Ronan remembered this history. He remembered. And so, he smiled as her saw her, glistening in the moonlight, the early evening moonlight, and somehow, he sensed that she was both at peace and ready to strike at a moment's notice whenever She heard The Call.

From there, Ronan walked to the Old Royal Naval College. He sauntered over to King William Court that faced the Nelson Pediment, and there he saw a face – a woman's face – surrounded by red brick. He got closer, and she blinked. He looked again. She blinked. He looked closer, and then there was a sudden flash of light. Somehow, he was now in the watery depths – what was this place? He saw mer-men, mermaids, and mer-lions. He was walking on the seabed, and despite being engulfed by water, he could still breathe. He couldn't get it. He couldn't fathom it.

"What is going on? I don't understand!" he asked out loud, but quiet enough that no one heard him. "Where am I?" He saw carriages propelled by the fins of whales, dolphins, and other creatures of the sea. He walked further. Then he saw something strange. He saw people fighting, rather, sea creatures fighting. He could see a mermaid with a red belt of rubies and emeralds with a sword in her hand, and she was fighting a mer-man, but suddenly, she did not have a tail on her body, but human legs. Ronan guessed she must be one of the Aquaticans, who can be anything they can put their minds to. The mer-man and mermaid were fighting in sword-to-sword combat. Then, as the mer-man knocked the sword out of the woman's hand, they became engaged in hand-to-hand combat. The woman did pretty well, holding her own, but then came a series of blows – one to the chest, one to the face, one also to the lower body, and a kick between her legs. She was about to come crashing down onto the ocean floor when Ronan got involved. He never believed, no matter what a woman was like, that she should be beaten down like a dog.

He stepped in front of her and said, "Pick on someone your own size. You are an ass."

The mer-man's eyes glittered with rage, shining a type of purplish blue. "All right, you want to get involved – get your hands up. Be ready to die."

Ronan nodded but knew differently. The two then engaged in hand-to-hand combat. Ronan swerved from side to side to avoid the mer-man's blows. Ronan later found out that this mer-man was Gergaen, one of the sons of the King Mer-Lion, Seragaen. Ronan's punches then connected, sending Gergaen flying. He continued on with his attack, running up to Gergaen and punching him further. Then he kicked him before picking him up and throwing him.

He came close to finish him off before the woman grabbed at him and screamed, "Stop! Don't kill him. You can beat him to a pulp, but don't kill him."

Ronan stopped. The mer-man was about to get up and punch Ronan again while Ronan's back was towards him, when the woman jumped in and punched him out, sending him sailing into a wall of coral reef.

"That will do," she said. "He's just knocked out cold for a while. He will wake up eventually. Thank you for defending me. He caught me off guard. I was just walking from the shop of the faeries. I needed some coral dust. I don't even know him, not really. He is the Prince, but I have no business with him. Maybe he thought I was someone else. Anyway, thank you."

Ronan nodded. "I am also not from these parts. I am looking for lodging, a place to stay. Do you know of any?"

The mer-woman nodded and took him to the local tavern. There they had sumptuous but simple rooms, which is why they only demanded a small fee. "You will need corae for money. Do you have any?"

Ronan shook his head.

"Well, here is some. A small thank you, I know, but here it is."

Ronan was grateful.

"You, are you… from here?" asked Ronan.

"Yes… and no. I'm on my way to another land – Another world – Tír na nÓg. To the land of Mystics and Faerie. I have a calling there. Someone I have to meet. I might need company — a consort, if you will. Would you be interested?"

Ronan agreed, nodding his head. The next day, they set out for Tír na nÓg. Ronan later found out that the woman's name was Gabrienne. The two walked through another gateway — a vermilion door — and came across a violet gold light and a Yew Tree that was part of a chapel in an area, near a lake, called Muckross.

The abbey was Muckross Abbey, frequented by Franciscan monks known for helping people, showing kindness, and compassion. There was a cat there who was really a woman, descended from a people who shape-shifted into cats when necessary. She had green eyes and nodded at them when they came close.

"I was expecting you," she said quietly. She pointed her hand toward the tree, and they followed her. A green door appeared. They went in. Suddenly, all was quiet and black. Then there were pinpricks of light that pierced the darkness. Then, portals of vermillion, persimmon, emerald, and indigo appeared. The sky seemed to open up. They walked through.

There was a man with long jet-black hair riding on horseback. Somehow, Ronan knew that it was the Celtic hero, Cúchulainn, who travelled different worlds and experienced many conquests in battles. His legend spanned time and space, and Ronan knew that he would always have an unforgettable place in Story. Cúchulainn was on horseback, speeding toward a battle near a lake of dark cobalt, and he was fighting his best friend, Ferdia, in a fight to the death — swords, daggers, and shields locked in combat. Sparks flew from the clanging of metal against metal. In his heart, Cúchulainn saw Ferdia as a brother, and he was devastated. He had to fight Ferdia to the death for a bull – the Brown Bull of Cúailnge? Somehow, deep inside, he knew that this was wrong. But despite his gut instinct, he continued this disturbing hand-to-hand battle punctuated with blood, sweat, and the clash of silver and gold armour.

It was day. Then, it was night. It was day again. Then suddenly, surrounding them were four-legged creatures of silver and black fur with beady, red eyes glowing blood red. Their hunger was evident from the saliva dripping from their mouths – mouths that had sharp fangs ready to tear flesh. They were the Mocturna from the Other Side Of The Moon – the Verjandaes who lived in Lady Vertania's other mysterious and magical lair. The two fighters looked around.

"What is this?" asked Cúchulainn.

"I don't know," answered Ferdia, his best friend. "It's something unlike I've ever seen."

"These… creatures…?" whispered Cúchulainn, softly.

"Yes," said his friend. "They are from another world."

The beasts growled, saliva falling from their mouths as they bared their teeth, their eyes full of hunger and glowing an unforgettable red. They started to howl louder, and their numbers magically increased. Their fur, the colour of silver and black, changed into magenta and an unforgettable crimson. The two friends looked at each other. They quickly flew into action.

Cúchulainn started throwing daggers at the beasts and, as he closed his eyes, more swords and daggers appeared in his hands. He had often been to the land of Tír na nÓg and had received magical powers. His brother, Ferdia, had a similar ability and telepathically called swords and daggers, as well as a shield made out of the metal fashioned by elves, which appeared at his side. The two continued to fight off the beasts, but to no avail – there were too many.

Suddenly, Ronan, watching what was happening, knew what to do. He ran toward the two, quickly became a Mocturna, of Lady Vertania, of the Opposite Side Of The Moon, one of the Curandaes, and started fighting the beasts, growling and baring his teeth. He glared. He growled. The pack started to retreat. But two of the beasts became less timid and started to attack Ronan. He threw them off, hissing and growling. Then, he became human, conjured up some daggers, and started throwing them at the beasts. One by one, they died, and the mob of beasts started to retreat.

From the side, Gabrienne, the mermaid from Atlantis, watched, but then she saw a wolf coming from behind to attack Ronan. Quickly, she yelled, "Watch out," and flew into action. She became a huge eagle and tore into the beast, pecking out his eyes and tearing into his flesh with her claws. This also made the mob retreat.

Cúchulainn and Ferdia breathed a sigh of relief. They had never encountered such things and were speechless. They thanked the two compatriots, Ronan and Gabrienne, and then decided not to continue the fight – there was another way to show honour to what was important, and the Brown Bull of Cuailnge was not worth it. Also, Ferdia discovered from Cúchulainn that the Queen of Connacht, who had convinced him to fight Cúchulainn, had lied. She told Ferdia that Cúchulainn said that he did not see beating Ferdia in combat as a worthy victory. That was not true. For those two reasons, their friendship was not worth the sacrifice. Ronan and Gabrienne agreed with their decision.

They thought it was a wise move and that the two brothers needed to reach the main battleground as soon as possible to help the rest of their countrymen. The situation was dire, and the hourglass was almost empty.

The four continued for awhile on the same road together, but then Ronan and Gabrienne parted ways with the fighters, for she needed to meet someone, and she wanted Ronan to meet her too. Gabrienne knew that it was meant to be, and that again, fate would intervene. Gabrienne was to meet Magda, one of the Tuatha Dé Danann. When Magda heard of what Ronan and Gabrienne did to save Cúchulainn and Ferdia, she was pleased but knew that Cúchulainn would come to another fate… his death, later on in life… Magda would try to change that, but she had a feeling it would be to no avail. But when the time came, she would try anyway.

But in the back of her mind, she thought she felt something, heard something – was she experiencing a déjà vu? Something was in the back of her mind, in the corner of her thoughts. Was all lost because she couldn't save this brave young man, this warrior, Cúchulainn? Was the intervention of these two not enough? Magda knew that sometimes Fate had her own will, and sometimes no matter what you do, the outcome is the same – no matter what path you take, the outcome is the same – so all she could do was to steer her own path. For all of eternity, Magda would try and save the Spark, the Lightning, that was Cúchulainn. For that was part of Fate too, being one of the Tuatha Dé Danann.

Chapter Twenty-One:
The Continuing Chronicles Of The Mocturna

THEO, son of Stephen and Gwen, who had settled in Londinium, went for an adventure on Lady Vertania. Stephen and Gwen were happy in Londinium after getting married, but their son, Theo, wanted to discover more of his roots – the Mocturna side of his heritage.

Theo walked the grounds of the Old Royal Naval College and entered a portal opposite the Nelson's Pediment, facing a woman's face surrounded by brick. He was suddenly in the realm of Lady Vertania, walking on the craters in a sea of stardust and the silk of the stars. One of The Mocturna appeared.

"What say you?"

"I am Theo, the son of Stephen and Gwen. I am here to learn more about my father's people."

"Oh, you are…? I don't believe you. You'll have to prove your worth."

"Oh," said Theo. "I was not aware."

"Bring back the pocket watch of your father and the thumb ring of your mother."

"But, why?"

"Do as you are told."

Theo nodded. He went back to Earth and asked Stephen for his pocket watch. Stephen gave it to him without question but arched his eyebrow. Theo then went to his mother, Gwen, and asked for her thumb ring. She also arched her eyebrow but asked no questions and gave it to her son. He then went back through the portal and gave it to the Mocturna, whose name was Thomas.

"Well, you did it. You are the son of Stephen, one of the Mocturna. You have to fulfill another task. You must get the golden scroll of Pucharaes. It was lost to us, and unfortunately, all the secrets she held have also vanished. We have been looking for this parchment touched by the elvish gold from across time, for many millennia. The Pucharaes, she has secrets illuminating mysteries about healing, passing through different worlds, and other mystical beings that are a part of our ancestral line but are not known to us because of the scroll's absence. To have her in our possession would be vital to the survival of the Mocturna."

"Where would I get this?" asked Theo.

"You must go to Andeira to get it. Go through the Orion's Belt, and there you will seek it."

Theo nodded and started flying through the universe. He went through another door – a violet door made out of oak. He talked to a dragon dressed in silver armour.

She said, "You are on your way. You are on the path. Here is a crystal ball. Good luck on your journey."

Theo thanked her and continued on. He then came across a Star Goddess dressed in robes of silk from Lady Vertania's realm.

"You are getting there," she said, smiling. The Star Goddess had ravishing auburn hair and sparkling green eyes, and she was wearing a wrap of amaranthine stardust and swatches of the dark black velvet of the universe. "Here is a tunic made out of the stars of the Milky Way."

Theo nodded and thanked her. He continued onwards, flying through the cosmos. Then, he came across a wall, a wall made out of drystone forged from meteors. It shone shades of magenta and gold. He climbed it. Then there was a forest of silver trees made out of nebulae. They sang and shook in the sparkling blue velvet of the cosmos. Sang and shook. Sang and shook. Sang and shook. The music was unforgettable, kismet, and reminded him of the chiming of bells. He was enraptured. He continued. Then, he had to climb a mountain made out of asteroids and shooting stars. A mountain pick appeared in his hand – feeling grateful, he smiled and continued climbing up the mountain.

At the top, there was a pyramid, a pyramid of silver and mauve. A door opened up, and he went inside. There was a faerie, a faerie with mahogany skin, that greeted him, wearing robes of silver and gold. He continued further. There was another faerie with the complexion of cocoa. He walked further and saw another faerie in all her splendor, with robes made out of stars and stardust. Her eyes twinkled mauve and sapphire, with a hint of ruby.

"You are here," she smiled.

"Yes, I am here for Pucharaes – the golden scroll. Where is it?"

"You are not patient."

"There is no time. I need it to find out about my history, my beginnings as Mocturna."

"Well, since you are in a hurry, then, let's get to it – let's not waste words. You must kill me to get it."

"I don't understand."

"You must kill me to get it."

"No," he replied. "I can't."

"You will…" The faerie pointed to an ominous pink cloud that suddenly appeared. It then changed into a sea serpent, one sparked into being by a meteor shower. The serpent was vermilion, gold, and amethyst. It started to slither about.

"I can't believe this," shouted Theo. "I can't believe that this is happening."

The sea serpent laughed and started to go after Theo. She started swishing around her tail to kill him and shatter him into a million pieces. He kept jumping, jumping, jumping… And then the tunic he was given, which had been tucked away in his leather sack, appeared and defended him by becoming a shield. Out of nowhere, his mother's thumb ring appeared and started shooting rays of light and fire toward the creature. The pocket watch then appeared and became a compass, directing him where to strike his blows and directing the rays from the thumb ring. The crystal ball also left his sack and became a sword that appeared in his left hand. Theo started to swing it left to right, right to left. He continued fighting until he got close to the serpent, then he drew his sword and cut off its head. But unfortunately, more heads appeared from out of the wound. He was dumbfounded and was about to give up when one of the heads came for him. Suddenly, the Star Goddess who gave him the tunic appeared – she was one of the guardians of this realm, and she became a unicorn. She used her horn to gore some of the heads of the sea serpent. The dragon that Theo had met earlier also appeared with her silver armour and breathed fire onto some of the other heads that sprang up. Then, a miracle – a Mocturna, a beast with red, blaring eyes and sharp teeth, appeared and attacked some of the heads of the serpent. Theo, who suddenly had more life in him, went for its heart. He transformed into a Mocturna, tore the heart out, and destroyed it. Then, the sea serpent disappeared. The woman, a faerie in silver and mauve robes, reappeared.

"You have done well," laughed the faerie. "You have defeated my creature. You deserve Pucharaes, the golden scroll."

"Thank you," said Theo. "Now, I am on my way, as this is the key to knowing who I am."

"You're right, son," said a voice. Theo looked to the right. It was his dad, Stephen. "Son, you have done well."

"It's you – you saved my life. I didn't know… I didn't tell you anything."

"I know," said his father, laughing. "But I knew you were up to something. I discussed it with your mother, and I went to the realm of Lady Vertania. I talked to Thomas, one of the brethren of the Mocturna. He told me, begrudgingly, about what you wanted – to know more about your heritage – and the challenge he gave to you to get that. A bit unfair, but that's who he is, and that is the way of the Mocturna. I had to make sure you came out all right." Stephen laughed again.

"Well, I –"

"There's nothing you need to say, son," said Stephen. "I think, though, it's time to go home."

"I agree," said Theo. "What happened… it was so unexpected."

"Yes," said Stephen with a twinkle in his eye, laughing. "It was, wasn't it?"

Father and son passed again through different worlds, ending up across from the Nelson Pediment that overlooked King William Court in the Old Naval College. The two faced the woman's face of stone surrounded by brick, but in this moment, she was silent, as the two Mocturna had already passed safely from the other world into the present one.

"I will tell you more about the Mocturna," said Stephen. "There is so much to tell you, like why I left that world to come here to start anew. I should have told you long ago, but I wasn't sure if you wanted to know about that part of yourself. There are not many who will understand. And if you want to go to the library that Thomas alluded to, to learn even more about your heritage, let me know. I will take you. You did not have to risk life and limb to do that."

"I understand that now, Dad, and I do want to know more. I won't tell anyone else right now, but I need to know for myself."

"Yes, I understand, I get it," said Stephen. "Let's go back, and I will tell you. Your mother will have words to add as well. She knows about that part of my life, and as she is married to a Mocturna, she will give you her perspective."

Theo nodded. And the Story Ends, but the Story also begins.

***

I am Magda… one Of the Three… The Raven is my symbol… My Mirror Self. The river… home to the golden salmon, the Salmon of Knowledge – we drew forth inspiration, as well as knowledge…

I have taken One, a Young One, from the isle of green to the desert and to the mystical land of Atlantis, but now, she must know her own Story; they tell me it is time. Raen is now Remembering.

The Water continues to Rush Forth…
The Memories come forth,

The Salmon   Swim FASTER

The   Golden   Salmon   Of   Knowledge

The   Golden   Salmon.

Chapter Twenty-Two:
Raen

I was thinking. I had travelled with Magda, the woman with two crows, rather ravens, one on each shoulder. We had been magically transported to the Sahara and then to Atlantis. I had met some other interesting women – Cara, Oceantis, Staerkie, and another woman who went by the name of Harriet. Her name sounded familiar, but where have I seen her face before? I'm sure when I talk to the others further, I'll know more about her Story. The adventures I am having already – I cannot believe what I am seeing. It feels like I am in a Dream. If only my girlfriend, Sheila, could see this. My thoughts surged elsewhere, and I continued to think of my life Before.

Before I got to Atlantis, this magical city underwater, I was in Dublin at a post office and looking at a tall statue of a hero from one of the Tales of this land, Ireland, known for its endless green. I am a doctoral student pursuing a PhD – the first of my family to go to university, the first of my family to get a Bachelor of Arts, a Master's degree, and now a Doctorate, hopefully. I want it, but it's not been easy, and I'm not sure if I'm meant to have it. My advisor said I'm doing just fine, but still, there are red marks all over my papers. She assured me I'm doing just fine, yet I don't know… maybe I should give up. Someone told me there are people who will tell you that you are not meant for these things, but we are meant for these things. Do not let anyone get in your way. Find a way to finish. Find A Way. I want to, I really do, but I feel discouraged – am I really meant to have this? Am I worthy?

I am remembering the doubts that I had before I got to Atlantis, but I have a feeling they will dissipate – why, I don't know. But I think they will disappear, will be drowned out. I am black, and I am Irish, but yet I walk between different worlds, as my mom is white and my dad is from the West Indies, one of the few West Indians who emigrated to Ireland instead of going to England. Why did my father go there? He wanted to do something different. He wanted to go on an adventure. His cousins all trained as nurses, but he decided he wanted to open up a fish and chips shop. People said he was crazy, but he had to prove them wrong – that's who he was. He's gone now, died… Cancer… It took him, this vibrant, brilliant man who could have done anything but decided to carve out his own path, not medical, and open up a fish and chips shop.

He took it over from an Italian family who had emigrated to Ireland years before. They took him in, adopted him, and gave him a place to stay in their house when no one else would. It was a village wary of strangers. Wary of a person with mahogany skin. He was one of the first, before people from various African countries came over to this land.

Me – I am of two worlds. My mother said, insisted, "You are Irish, you are a part of us."

Dad said, "You are West Indian, too, but there are

those who will not accept you because of the colour of your skin. But, Raen, you will find your way. You are like me and your mother, too – you will find your way. We will. We all do."

He would smile at me and tell me stories about ghosts, duppies. He was from Jamaica and told me about the Maroons… He told me about the Irish who started new lives on islands like Barbados. From across the seas, they often became a part of island life, building those new lives with people from other worlds because of love. He told me these things. And now, I am going to college and pursuing a PhD.

Now I am here, looking at this statue of Cúchulainn… Mom told me these stories about our Irish ancestors – she always wanted me to know that I was a part of it, and the Irish ancestors – we are all a part of it, no matter what anyone else says – for many of us are of more than blood and have more than one ancestral home. And as I continued looking at this statue, I was reminded of Something… Something… Maybe Mom was right – maybe she was. Are The ancestors calling? Are they –

"Yes, Raen," Magda said, as we were now in the library in Atlantis, where Harriet was reading a book, a book of bright emerald. "You, too, must read about your own story, which is part of many other Stories. It is now time to begin."

I nodded, and a book drifted into my hands, a book of bright magenta. This book called to me – this book that glowed with a bright cobalt hue. I opened it up and turned to the first page. And so, the Journey began.

I saw something shining bright – it flashed and then grew bigger. It was an orb of red light – the way to the

Land of Tír na nÓg. There was a flash, and I heard thunder; then, I closed my eyes. Swirls of sound surrounded me, and I descended deeper into the chaos of noise, deeper into the chaos of sound. I saw a tree, an oak, spanning as far as I can see, and there was a golden light. I fell, descending down, down, down into a hole – I felt like Alice, tumbling down into a magical world. A portal, I feel, just as I hear someone say, "It's a portal." There is wind, a rush of Sound and Colour – Sound, Light, and Colour… It's a Maelstrom, Halcyon, it's a Tsunami, and my body is falling further down the hole. It's a Freefall through Time… and then there is a Silence, and then there is Sound, and then there is Silence again.

I hear them say, "We are here. You Will Remember Who You Are, You Will Remember… Who You Are… You will Remember. And then there is another door, and it opens, followed by another of a dark aubergine, and then there is another door of emerald. Suddenly, I was walking through glass corridors brightly lit by the sun, and then, there was a gateway. I appeared in a forest. I saw something – a shape that I could make out as human as I walked closer. It was a woman of around five feet two inches, with jet-black hair and green eyes, but she did not see me, although I was so close. I was within walking distance, but she didn't see me and continued on her path through the forest. Suddenly, I heard thoughts – they were not mine, were they hers? How is this possible? Where am I? There was a low hum. I knew I had to keep walking and somehow, I would find the answers.

✷✷✷

Evain was a woman, a stranger to the village. She

worked hard to fit in, but to no avail. She said out loud in frustration, "What can I do to fit in, to find my place?"

Evain worked hard as a barmaid, doing what she could to earn her keep. She caught the eye of a handsome man, one who had money. They married, but he often kept her in terror – a prison, a gilded cage. She had fine clothes and a beautiful mansion to live in, but she had no value. She was the nightingale that was admired, taken out once in a while, but then put back in the cage. One day, she met another man – kind, tall, with jet-black hair and unforgettable blue eyes. She fell for him instantly, and he felt the same about her. It was kismet. It was fate. They became lovers. It was as if… she just wanted to be with him. They would take long walks in the forest, sparked by moonlight and the stars above. She felt that they were magic. But one night, her husband saw them and vowed revenge. Her lover was a tailor known for his craft, but her husband sent him on a job far away from home, to make clothes for a family he knew, and he had to be in that town, working at another shop to do the fittings. With him gone, Evain was vulnerable. She was driving the carriage one night when it stopped. She looked around – why were the horses spooked? She looked around again. From out of nowhere, a hand was around her neck. She was being choked, gasping for air, when a being appeared in a cloud of amethyst light – amethyst and gold light. The hand fell away, the carriage quickly jumped into motion, and Evain didn't look back.

The next day, she found out that her husband was dead. They looked for her, but she hid in the woods. Things started to happen. People would drive their carriages through the woods and hear her laughing, laughing – but it wasn't Evain. They saw carriage doors opening and closing, opening and closing. But it wasn't Evain. Unfortunately, one night, a mob came for her where she was staying – in a room above a tavern. The tavern keeper was away doing business in another town. The wife was there but mortified. She couldn't stop the mob. They had come for her. They had come for Evain. They took her and were about to hang her in the same forest where she walked with her love, the same one… Then, suddenly, there was lightning – suddenly, there was thunder – the lightning struck the mob. It struck the tree that Evain was about to be hanged from. She fell to the ground. Amazingly unhurt, she ran to a lake – Baylock – not far from the Golden Veil. Other people not hit by the lightning ran after her – she did not know what to do. She was afraid. They came closer. Closer. Evain jumped into the lake – it was shallow at the edge, but the further she waded in, the deeper and deeper it got. She started to drown. But suddenly, there was a Light – a Light Of Deep, Luminous Lavender surrounded the lake and almost blinded those from the mob who got close. Frightened, they ran away. The Light surrounded Evain. She thought she was dead, but no – it was like she was rising and then floating above the water. Floating. Floating. Floating.

Evain was then taken away to one of the beehive huts not far away – it was a portal to another world. She flew through and ended up in a place with a huge sphinx of limestone. There were formations in the shape of a triangle, also built entirely out of limestone. What were they called? She was trying to remember… from school… Pyramids? And there were some women, beautiful women, with mocha skin shining in the light – others with a sheen of mahogany or light-coloured sand. They had gorgeous headdresses of fuchsia and emerald. They welcomed her.

"Evain," they said. "Welcome home. You are a part of us. You no longer have to run."

Evain then became another Sister, one who is a part of this Womanhood, one of the leaders of the army of the Automatons of Bubastis, The City Of Cats, where Queen Amanirenas reigned along with Odae, leader of the Aziza, and also had as a fellow Sister, Hypatia, an astronomer and mathematician. Evain also became an Engineer, Soothsayer, and Wise woman, as when she was a child, she was an avid reader, because her Aunt had her own personal library, one of the few in her village. Evain was happy in the City Of Bubastis. She worked with other peoples, such as the Dogon People from Mali, and also those from the Kush empire, led by Queen Amanirenas. There were artists, astronomers, mathematicians, and engineers, people of all various shades – mahogany, cocoa, and ebony. Evain was helping to forge a new Sisterhood. Evain had found a way from the watery depths of Baylock to this – the City of Bubastis. And she, Evain, was also akin to the watery kingdom that was Atlantis, the realm below the Eye Of Africa, working with the Mer-lions there. So Many Stories… So many stories… Running through time.

***

Fire. Black. Ebony. A fury of fire…

I, Raen, continued to read this book of magenta, mesmerized by the Mystic, and the pages, they were speaking to me, calling to me… voices… a crescendo, a verbal tsunami, a chaotic orchestra. They wanted me to know something – to see something, to learn something, and believe. The ivory pages continued to turn, and there were times that I did not need to even turn them, as they were Magic. It was all

About Story, and so I continued to delve into the Realm Of Imagination, reading the symphony of black and white.

Chapter Twenty-Three:
Magda

CHESS… a board made out of grass. The beasts – the Queen, the Lion, the Unicorn, the Dragon… and Others, but I remember the triad. The Triumverate. The Power of –

I was walking through lands of marble and pink ice, mountains of mauve – a land of Snow, A land of Rain… frozen water… Me, the one with ravens at my side, one on each shoulder – Me, Magda, one of the Tuatha Dé Danann, one of the three Warrior Sisters, daughter of my father, who is the King of The Ocean. I found this board, this magical, surreal chess game in a forest made out of silver and bone, the bone of dragons and wyverns. My sister, Claire, who was walking beside me, asked, "What is it?"

"I am tired. War, the Death of Cúchulainn… it haunts me, Sister. And I need to rest."

Claire nodded and said, "You must seek a different path for a while. Seek it, my sister." I nodded and started walking, Walking, Walking.

Years passed, and I still felt a longing for another life. I put some food in a sack, a sack of leather from a deer – a quick-footed one who had the spirit of flight, light, and love. I had tracked her for quite some time. We are all part of the Circle. We are all one, and one is all. I gave tribute to her as my arrow pierced her heart. I gave tribute to her by eating from her flesh and tanning the leather. I continued to pay tribute to her, thinking, "We are all a part of it, part of the Circle." I then continued through the forests of emerald, through forests of snow on the mountains from up high, passing by the chapel founded by Saint Fin Barre.

I continued and continued until I came to a clearing within the forest. It was a farm with sheep and cows. There was a calf of a creamy ivory colour, with a man tending it. He looked lonely. I saw his heart. He was a widower. He had no children. He was on his own. I felt his heart. I walked closer. I offered my help as a farmhand and a cook, as I had experience working the land, helping a family of farmers on one of my adventures, seeking solace after one of many battles that I had faced as a warrior. The farmer agreed. He took me in. I did various household duties, milked the cows, sheared the sheep, and tended to the chickens. I did these things. And so, I was part of his heart… and his bed. We were… It was a beautiful time. A wonderful time, just the two of us – the two of us in love.

One day, he said, "I'm going to town, the village. I must get some sundries for us. Stay, rest. You work hard, Tanaine. You work hard. Stay."

I did and rested. He went to town. In the village, he boasted of a beautiful woman, a strong woman, who tended to his livestock, his cows and sheep – an industrious woman, a hardworking soul, swift on her feet and with her hands. He boasted to the men in the village that she could outrun any horse, any animal on four legs. Two men of the local lord heard his careless words.

I was asleep. Suddenly, I woke up. The men came to the door. They pulled me out of our home. My Heart, he was devastated. He had no idea about the peril, the dangerousness of words. They put me in chains and took me to a cleared track in the wilderness. But there was a tent, a canopy, for the Lord, the local lord. He looked at me from his leather chair, wearing clothes threaded with gold and silver, emblazoned with the symbols of the unicorn, lion, and the dragon. His eyes stared right through me. The rest of the village gathered around. They gathered around. They gathered. They wanted me to race two strong stallions of black, and I was pregnant – I knew they would be twins. My Heart did not know about my pregnancy as I was not showing yet, but he had a feeling, as I was not as steady on my feet, and I couldn't keep my eggs and drink of barley down.

The lord shouted, "Run, lass! Fucaen said that you were the swiftest, could outrun even the fastest horse, any four-legged creature. Run. Run. Run."

I begged him not to, to take back this decree. I told him I was pregnant. I begged him, begged him, and the crowd from the village chanted louder and louder. I saw my Heart – they had him in chains and began to whip him. I did not know what to do, so I began to run.

Then, out of nowhere, there was a Flash of Bright Light. There was a unicorn, made out of silver from the finest elves, for elves were the finest blacksmiths. The unicorn flew to the ground. People were shocked, they did not know what to do – and then something happened. She disappeared. Then, another figure appeared – it was an angel, an angel of mauve in a suit of armour of the finest hue, shining, shining. The men, the guards of the lord, went for her, but she brandished her sword and chopped off their heads. Village people came at her, and she continued brandishing her sword. The lord summoned his druids, and they chanted, summoning dragons. They were at first clouds, then came into being, breathing fire. A shield of ruby and emeralds appeared and shielded her from the fire. I was in shock; I couldn't believe it.

"Come," she said to me. "Come." I stretched out my hand. Suddenly, I was on a unicorn of steel. My Heart was below, and as the woman in mauve armour pointed her sword at him, the chains disappeared. He started to float up in the air, and she beckoned to him with her hand. He shot up further into the air and joined me on the steed.

He whispered. "Sorry. I did not know the weight of my words. I am sorry."

I nodded, but still there were tears in my eyes. The unicorn, called Euclates, took all three of us up to a mountain. When we were close to the mountain top, the woman, the angel of mauve armour, was silent for a moment. Then she said, 'Sometimes forgiveness is warranted. You must know when."

I nodded and held my Heart's hand. When we reached the mountain top, she turned to us and said, "Take care of each other. Do not let this foolishness return. Take care of each other and give each other the utmost respect and love." We both nodded.

When we dismounted from the unicorn, we walked through a gate forged from glass made from sand blown upon by a dragon's breath. We continued on the path of gold. We continued. We met a griffin. He nodded at us. "Come," he said. "Come. She is waiting for you." And there she was – the woman, sister of one of the warriors, in a similar suit of armour but of gold, with wings. She was sitting on her throne. She was sitting.

"You, Magda, and your Sister, Claire – you two were looking for something. You were seeking something before you chose a different path."

"Yes," I said, "we were seeking the Crystal of Elixaen. We need to find out what course we should pursue, for we feel that a Storm is coming, a darkness. Perhaps that's why I felt weary, tired, a lack of desire to surge forth – to know that more is ahead, but to not have the will, that is what I felt. And so, I need to have clarity. Clairvoyance is not quite my gift. Claire, my sister – it is more her gift, and the others of the Tuatha Dé Danann.

"Say no more. I understand the thing you seek. But you – you forgave the one who put you in danger… unintentionally… That is a brave act. That it is. You will then receive the much sought-after crystal, the Elixaen. For Magda, you are a warrior, but you wanted to choose a different path. But that Path, you now know, was not for you – my sister, Verchantus, wanted to make sure that you got back on it. Sometimes, we need a bit of guidance; sometimes, intervention is needed… sometimes Destiny is not enough. Sometimes, a gentle hand…"

I nodded. So, a crystal appeared in her hand, one made out of diamonds and gold forged by faeries and dragons.

"Here is the Crystal of Elixaen. Use it well. Remember also that we can be a gentle hand, a gentle guide, but sometimes, even that is not enough. No matter how much we intervene, even though we know the truth, the result will be the same. You will know this in time." I nodded.

"As for you," she looked at Fucaen. You have seen the error of your ways. There is nothing else to be said."

He nodded. We walked out of her lair, the lair of a queen who we later found out was Queen Sercantaes, a woman with stark blue hair and eyes with the light shade of pink blossoms, and older sister to Verchantus, the woman who saved Fucaen and I. Verchantus escorted us from her sister's palace.

The younger sister asked, "What is next. What is next for you?"

"It is time for me to go back – be a warrior, as I was."

Verchantus nodded, smiling. "It is your Destiny, your true path." She walked off and said, "When you're ready, I'll take you to where you want to go." She then left us alone.

I turned to Fucaen with determination. I could feel it. He understood and said, "I want to join you. I have learnt the error of my ways, and I want to still be a part of your life. I will do better."

"Then, come with me." I put a hand on his cheek. And so, he did, becoming my soothsayer and collector of knowledge, as he loved books; it was meant to be. And as the clerk, the cleric of our archives, the Tuatha Dé Danann spells and histories, my Heart knew it all as he had learned the stories and the songs from his youth from his uncles, who were druids.

We both walked up to Verchantus and said, "We are ready."

She took us on her unicorn of steel, the woman in armour of now rose gold, and took us to my land – my home, home of my sister, and all who are a part of the Tuatha Dé Danann and the other Mystical Ones. From there, we would go on many adventures, with Fucaen guarding the realm of knowledge. We had twins, a boy and a girl.

Our girl learned to be a warrior, and our son followed the ways of his father, being a clerk, scholar, and druid. The Elixaen was in a special chest made out of oak, an oak tree guarded by the druids.

The sun was setting, becoming a red ball of fire. Who would know what would happen next? It was written in the stars. It would be decided by the gods and goddesses… the Mystical Ones that were a part of the Tuatha Dé Danann and beyond. Isis, from the other world, the land of pyramids and the Sphinx, she smiled and nodded. She knew about this Life, filled with twists and turns, and knew that wherever your next step will take you, awaits a Mystery.

Chapter Twenty-Four:
Angel

THE ivory pages continued to flip on their own, and my eyes – this doctoral student's eyes – were captured, entranced with every page. The Story Continued…

***

She was born out of the black orb of light and fire. She was the leader, the leader of the automatons. They wanted an endless energy source that would never diminish. One automaton, Taernelle, thought of what she could do. She talked to her Sisters, and they said, "Go to Tír na nÓg."

Taernelle did by entering a portal, an Oak tree, and talked to a guardian, a Faerie of Purple, a rich violet. She said, "Yes, you may enter." The automaton, Taernelle, did. There was a sunset of reddish gold. Then, it was night, pitch black. A dark blue velvet, speckled with stars. She continued. Then, she saw a tree. Then, another. She walked up toward it.

"What do you seek?" asked the tree.

"I didn't know trees could talk."

"Well, we can – don't you know you are in the land of

Tír na nÓg? Yes. You. What do you seek?"

"I seek endless energy for when we travel to different worlds to engage in battle with our enemies, where we can't teleport telepathically."

"You seek the Stardust of Sevantaes. You must go to the cave. The cave of dragons to seek it. There, you will find it. You will."

Taernelle walked many miles, and she even crossed deserts. She continued. Then she went to a cave. She entered and saw the dragons. There were four. She then saw the egg that was the Crystal of Infinity. She got closer. Then a wall of glass brick appeared in front of her.

"Ahhh," said a voice. "You seek the Dust of the Celestial Ones, the Stardust of Sevantaes."

"Yes," said Taernelle. "I do."

"Well, you will have to answer one question to get her."

"What kind of question?" asked Taernelle.

"Listen, and you will know."

Taernelle nodded, knowing she would have no choice but to listen. A dragon suddenly appeared in front of her eyes, gleaming a bright indigo and mauve, and began telling his story.

***

Once upon a time, there were two ravens. One was small when she was born and was like that all her life, but her sister was much bigger and more desired, more sought after. They lived in a coven, in a nest, on an island. The ravens were shape-shifters, often becoming human, elf, faerie, or whatever they desired. The parents were the King and Queen of Devanaes. Their realm stretched out far and near. One day, an egg of theirs — a golden egg, the Verilium — that was purported to have a magical raven inside, one not seen in their lifetime, was taken. The King and Queen were devastated. The menfolk, the men of Devanaes, went searching for the egg. They came across a spider. Some were eaten. The rest of the men came across a dragon. They were eaten. The remaining men came across a sea serpent. The last of them were also eaten. The King and Queen, when they heard the news, were devastated. What were they to do? Who would retrieve the golden egg? The small raven, Rachael, one of their daughters, decided to take action. Yes, she was small, not favoured like her sister, Lanelle, but she wanted to do something. She set out as a human from the castle, not far from the coven, to another world where she would get the egg.

She first came to a stream. She saw the magical fish, the Salmon Of Knowledge. They said, "Go to the lair of Zercandaes, and walk on the rainbow. You will then see a golden harp. Take it with you." Rachael nodded. She walked through the valley of light and shadow, with large eagles flying overhead. But they meant her no harm, and she continued on her journey. When she saw the rainbow, she walked on it — it seemed endless, but eventually she saw the end with the clouds of white above her and a shining harp sitting on a mushroom. As she got closer, the harp started to play music. She was singing to Rachael sweetly, and when Rachael picked her up, she continued her melodic harmony. It was meant to be. Rachael continued on her way.

The harp then started to talk. "Rachael," she said. "You must talk to Magda, who is the Sister of Brigid. Brigid is the Goddess and Protector of all Storytellers and Bards and is one of the Tuatha Dé Danann. Magda, who is also part of those kin, will tell you what to do next."

Rachael nodded. She continued on her Path. She saw a forest of trees, mainly oak, but she saw one, a Yew tree. She walked up to it. A doorway of light appeared. She walked in. She was then skyrocketed amongst the stars. There was a mirror. She looked in it. She saw a spider. Then, she saw a raven. Then, she saw a swan. She shook her head.

"You are all of these things," said the harp. "Walk through." She did. Rachael saw more stars, and then she saw a library. She walked through the doorway. Books were shining, and they were creating a beautiful music, which the harp joined in. The orchestra of books and the harp put Rachael to sleep. When she woke up, she was floating above a table of oak, and there was a druid there.

"You wish to help your people? You wish to get the golden egg?"

"Yes," said Rachael. "I know I'm not the mightiest — I am small, not the brightest, but I have a big heart, and as much as I can, I don't give up."

"Yes, child," said the druid, "I see that. You have come a long way. Here is a book. It will help you on your journey."

"Thank you," said Rachael. "This means a lot to me."

"You're welcome. Go this way —" He pointed to a green door that suddenly appeared behind him. "I will see you again."

Rachael nodded but wondered what the druid meant. She walked through the door and, still thinking about it, she continued.

Up above, she saw wyverns and a clock. Suddenly, wyverns were flying at her, and they seemed menacing, but then one wyvern appeared in front of her, shielding her from the others.

"She will not harm you. She is not a danger to you." The wyverns stopped in mid-flight and looked at the violet wyvern defending Rachael.

"Are you sure?" asked one of the wyverns who was a dark grey. "She is not of our world. I think she is a threat."

"No, Romudalaes, she is not. She is here to help us. She seeks the Verilium, one that would protect our world and give us unyielding amounts of light to shield us from the darkness, so we can read our books and continue to give our people knowledge."

"So, are you?" asked the one who is Romudalaes.

"I guess so," said Rachael. "I'm willing to help you if you help

me. I am looking for the golden egg, the Verilium. It is from the realm of my Kingdom, but if it can help you, I'm sure we can come to some kind of arrangement."

Romudalaes nodded. His brother, the one who defended Rachael, Arthemaes, agreed. "Let's go with Rachael and help her find the Verilium."

All of the wyverns, their army, left with Rachael, leaving those who were the guardians of time and knowledge with The Clock, another portal that watched over Space And Time. The wyverns, some heliotrope, some ebony, joined Rachael on the pilgrimage. They continued, walking through different lands — some desert, some forest, even a land of periwinkle mushrooms. They continued their Sojourn. Soon, they came across a land of mirrors. They had to answer a riddle to enter.

"What is small but unyielding and unrelenting?" asked one of the unicorns who guarded the land of mirrors.

"The heart — the human heart," answered the wyvern.

"That is correct," said the unicorn. "Pass through."

And so, the whole group did. When they got to the end of the land of mirrors, there was another unicorn.

"What transcends time and space, can be papyrical, but also can fly like wings on the wind, in the air, from the mouth?"

"Story," answered Rachael.

"Yes," said the unicorn. "You may leave this world and enter another."

Suddenly, a shield of shining gold bejeweled with rubies appeared in Rachael's hands. The group went through the gateway. Then, they were in another land, where one man entered and bathed in a lake, came out again as a boy, then, becoming a man again. He stayed that way, timeless, throughout time. Swans swam on lakes of liquid crystal, and angels sang with birds, sitting in trees of glittering silver, talking to owls, and conversing with druids.

Rachael and her friends came to a clearing with no trees, angels, or druids. But there was a Voice.

"Rachael," it said. "You are here. You are here to take the Verilium, which gives endless power and energy…you… of the Realm Devanaes, shape-shifters and ravens, you. To do this, you must do One Thing."

"What is that?" asked Rachael.

"You must kill me."

"I won't. That is wrong. I won't."

"To get the Verilium, you must." The voice insisted. It was the voice of Magda, one of The Tuatha Dé Danann, but Rachael did not know that.

"No, I won't," said Rachael.

"Then, you won't get the Verilium."

Rachael was resolute. "No," she said.

"Then, you will have to battle with…"

A dragon appeared, with seven heads and seven crowns. A woman then appeared with the sun behind her and the moon, Lady Vertania, at her feet. The dragon came towards her, and fire came out from all directions. Rachael didn't know what to do. But then she remembered the unicorn gave her a shield for answering the riddle. She used it to protect herself from the fire. She continued. The dragon started to speak in a strange language.

A book appeared in front of her, translating what the dragon said. It was the book given to her by the druid. She was no longer in the dark. She nodded, and a bright orb of light surrounded her. She continued.

The fire was unrelenting, and the many heads of the dragon got bigger, but she was unafraid. One head came at her, and a sword appeared in her hand. She cut off that head. She continued cutting off other heads that came at her. She was unafraid. She wanted that golden egg, the Verilium, not just for herself, but for the new friends she made on the way. The woman with the sun behind her joined in the battle, and embers of light became spears that attacked the dragon. The wyverns jumped into the action, attacking the many-headed beast. Some of the wyverns shapeshifted into dragons to confuse the creature. Some angels saw what was going on and joined in the battle as well.

Another such devious dragon appeared, and the Army Of Light attacked and destroyed it as well, but out of nowhere, an eagle of gold appeared and went right for Rachael, taking a bite out of her arm. She started to bleed profusely, but other eagles appeared, wanting to help, and the Army of Light jumped into Action.

Wyverns, angels, and other mystical creatures appeared out of nowhere and helped. Even the owls previously in conversation with angels took part in the fight, and the druid who gave her the book also lent his assistance by becoming a fire-breathing dragon. Then Another appeared in the clearing. Quickly, this raven changed into a unicorn powered by a black orb of energy that spewed fire and heat and flew right for the gold eagle. The unicorn suddenly shapeshifted into a woman, and as a sword appeared in her hand, she sliced the eagle's head off. There was a round of cheers. Rachael had woken up, her body soaked in blood, with angels around her. They had started to heal her. On one side of her, looking down, was a tall woman with flaming burgundy hair.

It was her Sister, Lanelle.

"You're here," gasped Rachael. "I didn't know that you knew…"

"I had a feeling and knew I had to find you. You could not do this alone. It wouldn't be right, leaving you fending for yourself from all these things on your own. I'm sorry I wasn't a better Sister to you. I should have supported you a lot more. Then, you wouldn't have felt that you had to prove yourself and come on this journey alone. Forgive me, Sister."

"You are forgiven, Sister," whispered Rachael, who was suddenly feeling much better. Not only was the serum from the angels helping, but the soothing comfort of her sister's words did as well. "I feel stronger now. I can keep going now. The dragon, that beast—"

"It's finished. It's destroyed, as is the other. I have never seen anything like it. Dragons, for the most part, are kind, sympathetic, and compassionate."

"I know," said Rachael. "It surprised me too. That's why the wyverns can also shape-shift into dragons—they are a close friend and cousin to them."

"There is so much we do not know," sighed Lanelle.

"We will learn more in time," said Rachael, determinedly.

"Yes, you will," joined in Magda. "I am impressed, Rachael. You have done well. You were not afraid. You were not willing to fight me, but you fought the dragons, Zernzi and Zernzu. I had a feeling you would not fight me, but I knew you would fight them."

"You conjured them, didn't you?'

"Yes, I did," laughed Magda. "I knew you had a moral compass and would not fight me. Yes, I was right. You are welcome to Tír na nÓg any time."

"Thank you," said Rachael. "Let us go home, Sister. Before that, I would like to introduce you to my friends."

"I would like that," laughed Lanelle. "The more, the merrier."

And so, the sister met the other wyverns more formally—she had met many on the battlefield, as Rachael knew, but wanted a better, more fitting introduction. The group made their way back through the land of mirrors, answering more riddles, back to the realm of the Wyverns, and Rachael telepathically asked her parents if they could share the Verilium with the Wyverns there.

The King and Queen said, "Yes."

And so, a part of this golden egg was given to the wyverns so they could have never-ending light to read their books—stories, my-

thology, philosophy, astronomy, mathematics, art, physics, and so on — anything that was a part of their library. After all, what was the use of a library when they couldn't read? The wyverns were grateful. Yes, they were magical beings and could use fire, but their source of fire was not endless, and that effort would be for nought. This way with the Verilium, there would be never-ending energy. They were so happy and grateful for Rachael's help. The sisters went home to Devanaes and told their parents about their adventures.

The Verilium was an infinite supply of energy to power their automaton systems when they shape-shifted into automatons. No longer would they have to telepathically tell their metallic bodies to reboot when needed. Now, when they engaged in battle as unicorns forged from elvish steel, they no longer would have to think of mechanics when they travelled through time. The parents, the King and Queen of this realm, also decided that they should show Rachael more attention and treat both children more equally. This should always be the way. Rachael and her sister grew into powerful but compassionate warriors and knowledge seekers, often working with the wyverns to keep their worlds and the rest of the universes safe from evil and destruction.

***

"And so, Taernelle," asked the dragon, "do you understand?"

"I think I do," said Taernelle. "Anything is possible, and we do not do anything alone."

"Yes," said the dragon, his eyes beaming with a green and purplish light. "Yes."

The Stardust of Sevantaes suddenly appeared in her hands, and Taernelle flew back to the realm of Queen Amanirenas, the City Of Bubastis, and gave the Queen the beloved stardust. It sparkled and shimmered in a flask of diamonds fashioned by the faerie artisans. Taernelle also told the Queen what she had seen. The Queen nodded, for she understood the Power Of Story.

Chapter Twenty-Five:
Seranaes And Crysaes

THE book was ending, the one of magenta, but there was still one more chapter, one more entry in this mystifying book. My eyes continued to be mesmerized by each ivory page…

***

Unicorns… chessboard… Swirls of fire and flames… She saw her in the sky – a flying ember of green and gold.

"What is she?" asked a unicorn, small, gangly, but with a brave spirit.

"I don't know," whispered another, a mirror sister to the first unicorn. "I wonder – mother and father said that it's coming. What? I don't understand."

The two unicorns walked into a field. Suddenly, light, flame, and fire appeared in front of their eyes – three Beasts, creatures of a mystical sort… a lion, a unicorn, and a dragon. The two unicorns looked at each other.

"What is it?" asked the one with a symbol of a flower on her cheek.

"I don't know," replied the other. "It's something I had never seen before."

"Come," said the Lion with a crown on his head. "Come. I have what you seek."

The tall, gangly unicorn called Seranaes looked at him. "How would you know what I would like? You don't know me."

"You will be surprised," laughed the lion. "Come closer."

She did, and an aura of gold surrounded her and the lion. She hesitated but came closer – it didn't make sense, no, it didn't, but she had to.

"You want freedom – you want agency. You do not want to be a unicorn that is only being an appendage to someone else's dreams, someone else's adventures. You want to be the centre, the heroine of your own story."

"How would you know?" whispered Seranaes. "I don't know you."

"But I know your heart. We are all the same, in the end – we all have the same desires, the same needs and wants. You do not want to be like the others. You long for a different life."

"Yes," said the other unicorn, which would be Seranaes' sister. "Yes, that is what she wants. And I desire that too. This village, this glen where we are – Mom and Dad said that we have to be a certain way, but this way is not our way, and we feel that we are suffocating. It is time for something new, but we don't know how to get there. What else is out there? We just don't know, and we would like the opportunity to find out. But how?"

"I can help you," chuckled the lion, who was from the realm Turnaedon. "I can help you with that."

"And why would you help us?"

"Because the time has come… Because Destiny

calls… Because the worlds must unite. There is a darkness coming, and we must all become a Collective Force – all our lives are at stake."

"Really? Can we believe you?"

"You can't really," said another. It was the unicorn of silver. "You can't. Sometimes, you just have to trust. It's about faith."

Crysaes looked at her twin sister – she was only older by the emptying of an hourglass. "I just don't know."

"I do," said her sister, Seranaes. "I do. I trust. It doesn't make sense, but it makes sense to me. To Keep Going, to seek what we desire, we sometimes have to take a chance – a leap of faith."

"All right," said her sister, Crysaes. "If that is what you want to do, I support you."

Seranaes turned to the lion. "We are ready. We will take the leap. It's time to leave this glen – it is now a prison – and it is time to forge our own Path. What do we do?"

"You have already begun," said the lion, laughing. "Look at your right hoof." Seranaes did. She gasped. It was a beautiful bell made out of crystal. "It will give you clarity on this journey you seek."

Seranaes nodded. So did her sister. Seranaes then looked down again as there was a burst of light. There was a scepter in her left hoof.

"That will give you guidance on your journey; you will know what to do." Seranaes nodded. There was another burst of light. It was a Sphinx and an Ibis.

They both said, in unison, "You must not tarry. You must hurry." They then disappeared. The two sisters nodded, thanking the lion, the unicorn, and the dragon; they also nodded their heads in return. Before the sisters knew it, they had all disappeared.

The two twin sisters reappeared on a big chessboard in the sky. There was a piece in the form of a knight, and also a Queen.

The Queen suddenly became animated and said, "Continue. You are on the right Path." The two sisters nodded, riding on a comet and then waves of stardust. They passed by a nebula of gold, persimmon, veridian, and a beautiful cerulean. They opened up their mouths in surprise, aghast at the beauty. They continued riding the wave. They continued. Then a door opened up, of diamonds and crystal made by the rays of the moon and the dust from the stars. The door emanated a beautiful violet. They opened the door and went inside. There was a beautiful field, and in the middle of it was a knight.

"Hello," he said. "Who are you?"

"We seek a way to carve our own path, to be what we want to be. Agency is the grail we seek."

"I see," said the knight. "For your honesty, here is a flute, made out of the willow grown by the faeries of Gerantelus. She will give you hope amongst the storms."

The two sisters thanked him. He then said, "Go through that gate."

A gate appeared with the symbol of a mer-lion. They knew that it was the symbol of royalty, of the Mer-lions of Atlantis. They walked through, and suddenly, there was an ocean. They started swimming through, and it wasn't a struggle — the scepter not only shone a light but created a bubble around them so that no water would interfere with their movement. They travelled effortlessly through the ocean of stars and diamonds. When they got to the castle under the ocean, another gate opened up. It was one of seaweed and coral, but also gold and rubies. The same symbol of the mer-lion was on this gate. They continued and moved through the gateway. Once inside the grounds of the castle, the bubble floated up to the top of the castle and easily went through the castle walls. The bubble then disappeared, and the two unicorns, the twin sisters, walked up the twisting staircase of stone. They clip-clopped slowly, not wanting to fall, as it was a steep staircase, and one wrong step would send anyone easily to their deaths, falling into the depths of darkness below. The two continued up the staircase. Once at the top, they entered a chamber where the door of heliotrope was already open. The two went inside. A voice greeted them from the darkness.

"What do you seek?" asked the voice.

"We seek agency, being able to carve out our own life, not being dictated by anyone because we are unicorns, unicorns of the female persuasion. We don't want to just weave carpets of dust from rainbows into coats for those who go upon our backs for their own adventures. We don't just want to give people advice on their journeys – we want to go on our own." Seranaes said this emphatically. Her sister nodded vigorously in response.

"I understand, being I was in a position similar to yours. It's important to have agency. It's important to have your own journey. Yes, I understand. Come forward."

The two unicorns did so. At first, they saw nothing, but when they got closer, they gasped. It was a faerie, a beautiful one, wearing armour that emanated gold and emerald. She had a crown of vermilion, framed with diamonds and amethysts. But not only did she have golden armour, but she also had wings of the same metal, steel that Saraneas knew was forged by elves, for elvish steel was the strongest in all the universes. Not only did she have a fantastic body of armour, but she also had a shield with a large clock inside. Inset, it was also made out of amethysts. Her sword was on her hip, and her hair was an unforgettable flame of purple. Her eyes were a vibrant grayish blue. The two sisters had never seen anything like it.

"Yes, you are seeking something. You are seeking the Sword Of Terkandaes. This sword will not only give you agency, being able to create your own destiny, but you'll be able to cross over into other worlds, other periods of time, effortlessly. As unicorns, you are able to cross over into some worlds of your universe, but not others. With this, you can. Yes, you can."

"Why would you give this to us?"

"There is a royal line of unicorns, the Destinaes, that can do this. There is one that has been asking for you, being the Daughters of Lionus and Lekandaes. Your father was not receptive. He did not want his daughters to become warriors, but one from the line Destinaes heard The Call that you and your sister are meant to be a part of this line. Have you heard about any of this?"

"No," replied the two sisters together. "No," they repeated.

"I am not surprised. It is quite a request. Your father loves you, both of you, and does not, obviously, want his daughters to perish on the battlefield. But this one – she knows what your destiny is. She knows where the Story will go and how it will end. She knows that you two are a part of it." The two Sisters looked at the woman in golden armour in disbelief. They couldn't believe it. They – warriors?

"Yes, warriors. You two, warriors of the line Destinaes. Yes. To fulfill The Call, to become what you are meant to be, to be what you were already seeking, you will have to go to the One who beckons for you." The two nodded again. "You will have to go through the deserts of Mars. From there, you will find her."

"How will we know?" asked Seranaes.

"You'll know," said the woman, laughing, bedecked in the beautiful golden armour. "You will know. Good luck. I hope you find what you are looking for."

"Thank you," said Seranaes. "We will not give up until we find it. This is what we have to do. We do not belong in the Glen anymore. We have to Move On."

"Well, that is the hard part, but other challenges will be on your way. Go, and may Hera be with you." A unicorn of gold and violet suddenly appeared. She was made out of elvish steel.

"It is just my armour," answered the unicorn, smiling. "Let us go."

The three took off from the castle and flew through black holes, storms of comets, and passed through gales of asteroids. They came upon the planet of Red, Mars. They touched down and walked around. It was very cold on this planet as the winds had picked up, but none of the unicorns felt it as their aura protected them. They continued walking through the desert on Mars, bits of sand which forged with rubies, stuck in their hooves but magically disappeared because of their aura.

They came across a castle in the middle of the desert. The unicorn in the violet and gold armour took them through the gates. There was a symbol of a sword on the gates of diamonds and rubies. Once through, they had to walk across the moat as the drawbridge came down to greet them. Once across, they walked into the castle. It was unusual, as there were a lot of books floating in the air, looking like they were held up by invisible strings. Seranaes touched a book with her nose; she even touched above the same book with her hoof, but felt nothing. She was shocked – they were actually hanging in the air on their own.

"Yes, Seranaes, these books emit a type of magic. You will see in time," said the unicorn in the violet and silver armour. Seranaes nodded. Her sister followed behind. They came to a clearing in the floor.

The unicorn in armour said, "Stay, and close your eyes."

They did, and suddenly, circling around them were faeries of blue and green with long, gracious dresses and beautiful sashes of rainbow colours. The faeries pranced and spun around, their hands gesturing toward them. They continued to dance in a circle, faster and faster, and then suddenly, the three were rising up into their air, then skyrocketing to the top of the castle. Once there, they floated to a chamber at the top which had no staircase. Only by magic and by floating on a cloud of pink could they reach this chamber. Once near the door of silver, it opened, and then they went inside. The door closed quickly.

"You are here," said a voice, laughing. "You are here. Well done." The three looked around; they were in complete darkness. "Come closer," said the voice. They did. Once they crossed a carpet which they couldn't see, a burst of bright scarlet light greeted them, almost blinding the three. "Yes, you are here. Yes." Suddenly, they were facing a dragon – a dragon of vermilion with a tail of amaranthine. "You are here."

The three gasped. "You are in the right place. You seek

that Sword. Do not be afraid."

"I don't know if I can do that," said Seranaes, quietly. 'You are bigger than we are and more dangerous. You could easily kill us."

"I wouldn't, though," said the dragon. "That is not my intent. Instead, I show you the way to get the sword. That is the reason you are here, isn't it?"

"Well, yes," said Seranaes. "But we didn't think we'd be meeting a dragon. We were told about the line Destinaes. And then, we meet you. We don't understand."

"There is a lot we don't understand… a lot that does not make sense. But yet, we continue until things do make sense. It's about taking that first step, and then another and another, until we achieve what we seek. Sometimes, it is about faith."

"Yes, that is what a unicorn told us," gasped Seranaes.

"Yes," said her sister, Crysaes, quietly. "She mentioned that."

"She was right," said the dragon. "And so here it is… the way to the Sword, The Sword Of Terkandaes. You must go through this window, and once through, it will Begin, and you will get the Sword."

"Oh," said Seranaes' sister, Crysaes. "It's a riddle."

"Not really," said the dragon. "Just go through. You will know what to do."

Seranaes shrugged. So did her sister. The unicorn in the armour that was still with the unicorn twin sisters smiled, but did not say a word. She was sent to watch over these young ones. They did need some guidance, and the Queen in the golden armour knew that. "You will know what to do," said the armoured unicorn. "You will. Go through."

"You are coming with us?" asked Seranaes.

"No," said the unicorn in gold and violet armour. "I will not. This is your task, your journey. You two must go on your own. But you do have each other. That is all that you need."

"All right," said Seranaes. "We are ready."

"Then go forth, go through," answered the dragon of vermilion that also had a tongue of amaranthine to match her tail. "Go through, and good luck."

The two both nodded and went through, stepping through the window – instead of falling to their death, they were held up by a cloud of gold which formed into a staircase going up into the sky. Climbing up, up, up, the Sisters saw eagles flying in circles not far from the castle, and doves, as well as ravens. The Sisters continued climbing the staircase. It seemed to be forever, but obviously, it was not. The Sisters continued ascending the staircase. More birds, eagles, doves, and ravens. They continued up the staircase of golden clouds. Seranaes wondered when it would end.

"Sister," she said quietly. "Is this the way – is this how we will get the Sword?"

"That's what the dragon said," replied Crysaes. "I think we can trust her."

"Okay. I know we don't have much of a choice, but right now, I just don't know what to think."

"Sometimes, we just have to believe and take a chance. Sometimes, the brain, the mind, is not the key… Sometimes, we have to go on something else. This is one of those times."

"Okay, Sister, I guess I'll just keep going."

"Yes, just keep going. We'll get a sign soon."

They kept clip-clopping up the staircase. Finally, they

got to the top. When they were there, there was nothing. At all. No chamber. No other room. Nothing.

"What do we do?" gasped Seranaes. "There's nothing here."

"I just don't know what to say," said Crysaes. "I thought we would see some kind of sign."

"It's not looking too good," said Seranaes. "What do we do now?"

"You know what to do," said a voice. The sisters turned toward it. It was two birds – one an eagle and the other a dove. "You are in the right place," they said together, their voices chiming together like bells. "You are. Come with us."

"How?" asked Seranaes. "There is nothing here."

"You can fly," said the two.

"I know," said Seranaes. "But to where? We don't know where to go."

"We'll show you. Come now."

Seranaes looked at her sister. Her sister looked back. Seranaes knew what her sister was thinking – they were very close in age, being only a couple of grains of sand apart from the emptying of an hourglass.

"We'll come with you," said Seranaes. Her sister nodded in agreement. The two took off from the top of the staircase and flew with the dove and the eagle. A raven joined them on their flight.

Seranaes was not quite trusting of ravens. One had a grievance with her, which she did not understand. The raven had nipped at her neck and tried to chip at her horn. Seranaes fought back and batted the raven away with her hoof. The raven came back at her, but Seranaes used her horn to blast a ray of light at her, which killed her dead. It was self-defence. Her sister rushed to her side, not hearing about the struggle, as she was talking to an owl that lived in a yew tree. The two flew quickly to Seranaes' side, but she was okay, just a little rattled. Suddenly, a flock of ravens – one unicorn called them a "murder" of ravens – flew at the three. Seranaes was scared, but surprisingly, not her sister or the owl. The owl transformed into a large serpent, and her sister transformed into a much bigger unicorn – the two fought off the large flock of ravens, and they never came back to the glen again. Seranaes knew there were ravens that were not like that; there were those showing kindness and compassion but the memory of that raven – she would never forget.

As if the sympathetic raven read Seranaes' mind, she said, "I'm sorry for what happened. That was wrong. I heard about that – I knew you were defending yourself. That raven was envious of unicorns, especially of your wings and your horn… the horn had a special meaning for the raven. It is a symbol of transformation and magic, things that we ravens don't have – not in that way. We have many gifts, but they are different from yours. This raven did not quite understand that. She was envious, jealous of you. Again, I am sorry. You did not do anything wrong. The elders knew that, and from that point on, no raven was ever allowed again in your glen, your realm. They insisted. Your parents, the King and Queen of your realm, did not have to tell us – our elders made that decision to keep the peace. That was unacceptable, what had happened."

"I accept your apology," said Seranaes as they were flying. "I accept that. Thank you, for I did nothing wrong. I was just reading at the foot of the oak tree, minding my own business."

"I know," said the raven. "One of our elders saw the whole thing unfold. Nothing was missed. I want to help you and your sister on your journey. I insist."

"I accept your help," said the unicorn. The two continued to talk and fly, fly and talk, until they came to a big chessboard, a chessboard in the sky. Seranaes saw two chess pieces – the lion and the Queen. The Queen spoke up, and when she did, she turned into a faerie of blue.

"You are here. It is time." The lion, the other chess piece, nodded, turning into a real lion with a mane of red and gold.

"You will know what to do," he said.

Both sisters had swords appearing in their hooves. They were then standing on their two hind legs, but then something happened. They became human beings. Seranaes gasped. She didn't know they could shape-shift into human form. They could transform into faeries, elves, even mushrooms, though Seranaes didn't know why about the latter, but never human beings. But there they were – light sparkled around them, light and stardust. Seranaes became a redheaded woman, and her sister one with shining raven-black hair. The two both had purple eyes. Their legs were covered with leather, and their tunics were made out of leather, bone, coral, and stardust. Their swords were both made by the Elves of Sundore.

Out of nowhere leapt a unicorn made of a metallic red, and whose breath was at first black and then became a dark vermilion. Seranaes figured out that the stones of black emitted heat, which animated the creature. She had read about it, as elves often used these black orbs to heat things and used them to power their forges.

Seranaes still couldn't get over the fact that this unicorn was entirely metallic, made out of a shiny steel – a steel forged by some very talented elves, she figured. This unicorn was different from the unicorn that only had metallic armour. This one's body was made entirely out of this elvish steel. Her wings were also metallic. On the left side of her was a dragon, a dragon made out of the same steel and powered by the same black stone. A hot ball of fire came out of the steel dragon – the same breath as the unicorn. Seranaes had to jump out of the way. Crysaes, her sister, also had to swerve out of the way of the unicorn.

Both were weaving in and out, bobbing and weaving in and out so they would not be burned alive or decapitated. It was not an easy thing to do. They continued to bob and weave. Bob and weave. Then, Seranaes had an idea – she closed her eyes, and the flute appeared. The flute made out of willow from a tree that was part of the Fercantaes, a Mystical Forest that also gleamed with crystal and diamonds as well as rubies. There was a group of faeries who lived in the forest and were the guardians of that magical realm. Seranaes remembered that as she started to play a harmonic, haunting tune.

The unicorn forged out of metal started to close her eyes. The dragon seemed immune to the song, but the metallic unicorn started to close her eyes. Seranaes jumped into action. She had her sword and came at the unicorn and chopped off her head, as the sword could penetrate elvish steel. The head fell to the ground, which was made out of hard marble. Then, Seranaes jumped at the dragon made out of the same steel and tried to do the same. He grabbed hold of her and threw her off, slamming her onto the ground of marble. Seranaes was out cold. Her sister, Crysaes, screamed, running to her, but to no avail – the dragon closed his eyes and breathed out a bubble of emerald, which surrounded Seranaes' sister and held her prisoner. No matter what she tried, she couldn't escape. It looked like the sisters were done for. What could they do?

The dragon laughed and went toward Seranaes, wanting to eat her for his dinner. He opened his mouth wide and came closer to Seranaes when, out of nowhere, the unicorn with the armour of violet and gold flew in front of him.

"Noooooooooooo!!!!!!!!!!!!!!" she said. "Out of my way – you will not have her!"

The dragon laughed, undeterred. He continued to come closer, at which the unicorn closed her eyes and became a woman donned in mauve armour with wings. Seranaes could not believe it.

"How can she? How can she?"

"I can," said the woman, who was their friend and guardian now donning mauve armour. She was communicating with Seranaes telepathically. "I can. Watch."

She put out her hands, outstretched, and closed her legs, forming a cross. The helmet on her head grew wings, one on each side, small ones, but they both shone like the sun. Her wings grew bigger. She then began to sing, which entranced the dragon and started to put him to sleep. Then she started to fly around him in a circle, faster and faster, faster and faster, putting him in a tailspin. She kept doing that while singing, and then she stopped – flying away from the halcyon that was the dragon; she opened up her eyes, and threw her sword at the spinning dragon, the maelstrom of carmine. The sword went through and caused an explosion. It went Ka Boom, and the dragon burst into a thousand pieces, forming flying pieces of crystal.

Suddenly, the woman in mauve armour disappeared into the clouds above. The pieces of the crystal fell onto the ground, and then, something happened. The pieces reformed themselves, becoming azure instead of carmine, and they started to spin, faster and faster, faster and faster. Then, suddenly, it became an orb of bright, azure light. It rose up into the air and then descended to the ground. When the crystal reformed itself, it became the woman in the mauve armour who suddenly turned back into the unicorn of violet and gold. She looked back at Crysaes, then smiled at Seranaes.

"You two needed help. I was here. You have more than passed the test. You were brave. You were true. Here it is – the Sword of Terkandaes. Here it is."

The Sword appeared in the unicorn's right hoof. She was about to give the Sword when out of nowhere there was a burst of light – it was the raven that Seranaes thought she had killed. She came close to the unicorn of violet and gold. Seranaes, revived, quickly closed her eyes, and the Sword in the unicorn's hoof transformed into a crystal wall, protecting the unicorn from the raven. Seranaes did not want to kill the raven, wanting to give her another chance, but she kept coming at the unicorn in violet and gold armour, making big cracks in the wall – soon, she would break through it. Seranaes closed her eyes; she knew what she had to do. She came over and put an orb around the raven, hoping that would be enough. The raven, surprisingly, broke through and burst through the orb, flying right at Seranaes. Seranaes didn't know what to do, but then, another raven flew right in front of her eyes – it was her friend from before. She quickly put herself between Seranaes and the other raven, flapping her wings, rays of vermilion light emanating from her wings, killing the raven. Seranaes dropped to the floor in shock, not knowing what to think. The other raven, Tervina, her friend, became a human being for a moment and knelt down by Seranaes.

"Thank you for giving her another chance," said Tervina. "You are a kind soul. But sometimes, there are people or things that can't be redeemed – things that can't be changed. When that happens, you just have to let go."

Seranaes nodded, acknowledging a truth that she did not want to accept, but knew it was a part of life. She then sat still for a moment before getting up, as she had hit her head on the marble floor of the chessboard from the shock. Tervina, the shape-shifting raven, rested her hand on Seranaes' forehead, and she began to heal.

The unicorn spoke. "You three are all very brave. You, Tervina, you are the Best of the Dervinicus. You can also share in this sword." Another one appeared in Tervina's hands, as she was still human for the moment. "You are part of the healing. You are."

Everyone smiled. All four flew back down to the castle of the woman donned in golden armour. The two, the Queen being Servainius, and her sister, the unicorn in armour, Sercandisu, were indeed sisters, but Sercandisu preferred being in unicorn form, as she felt that was her true self. But sometimes, she would transform into a woman – she could even shape-shift into a dragon when necessary – whatever the situation called for. The unicorns with their Swords found they could travel, going through different worlds, not just traversing their own.

Tervina, the raven from the line Dervinicus, used the light of the sword to heal her people, as rays of that light would manifest as balls of crystal, so when anyone was near them, they would be healed immediately. This Sword Of Terkindaes could also copy itself into three swords, so three warriors from Seranaes and Crysaes' clan could travel through different universes, leading squadrons of the Sernikaes, the tribe of Seranaes and her sister.

The Sword would also emit a cloud of light, which could help others time-travel. Huge legions could therefore travel through time and space. The three, Seranaes, her sister, Crysaes, and Tervina, would meet once in a while, unite forces, and defeat evil in any galaxy or universe. The Queen in golden armour, called Servainius, as well as her sister, Sercandisu, would tell them about different goings on in the universes, and the three, Seranaes, Crysaes, and Tervina would help in any way they could, and because of that, many other people would heed the call. They would Heed The Call, and the Universes would Never Be The Same.

***

I closed the book, having read something that I had never encountered before. As a doctoral student, I had never come across something so inspirational. I, Raen, felt something that I had never felt before; I felt whole, almost completely whole. It was… I just don't know how to describe it. Having attended university for many years, I've read many books, done a lot of research, but ironically, I have never found what I was looking for – my own story, my own genesis. But, on this journey with these accomplished women – Magda, Harriet, Cara, and others – I was finally finding my way.

But still, there was something missing, and I saw it by looking into the eyes of that young woman, Cara, part of the group I joined in the desert. What was it? It wasn't

Harriet, the upcoming author. It was Cara, who had come from the land North of the 49th parallel – had I seen her before? She did look familiar, but from where? Somehow, I knew that I would find out what the answer was… Somehow.

The voices seemed to chime louder, louder, louder, and they said, "Yes, yes, yes, you will learn. You will know. You will –"

Acknowledgements

In bringing to life the universe of Harriet E. Wilson, there were many instrumental people who guided me on this journey. The American Antiquarian Society, who awarded me a fellowship that helped with my research about Harriet E. Wilson – I give thanks to this wonderful organization and the beautiful library that is housed there. Books are our friends. Also, I would like to mention Scott Casper, Nan Wolverton, and all who are associated with this inspirational organization that are a part of my Sisterhood.

I would also like to thank all of the supportive spirits from Hollins University, including Amanda Cockrell and Hillary Homzie. I remember and give thanks to Teresa Zackodnik from the University Of Alberta, who still encourages me on my artistic path.

I also give thanks to Adriana Davies, who guided me on my new endeavour, as well as Rona Altrows, Pierrette Requier, Joan Crate, Luciana Erregue-Sacchi, and Linda Harrison. Other supportive spirits include Amanda Lim for her encouragement.

I also would like to thank Yang Lim, Nadia Sadi, Yvonne Aldred, Susanne Goshko, Barb F. Schweger, Shawnna and

John Pracejus, Renee Gittens, and all of the Jordans, including Darren and Rose. Thanks also go to Lon Clarke, Diane Evelyn, Rudolph Wente, Leslie Schomp, and Mindy Buchanan-King.

For their never-ending support, I would also like to mention Carol Holmes, Giorgia Severini, the rest of the WGA, the Stroll Of Poets, Parkland Poets, Rachel Figeys, Cecilia Wyand, Jacqueline McNiel, Stephanie Ann Foster, Kelly Canner Pagano, Kris Stultz, Elsa Robinson, Tololwa Mollel, Michael Broodhagen, Sherry Skinner, Rose Brophy O'Neill, Shirley Romany, Jean Romany, Vernie Price, Joanne Wong, Deanna Chou, Tee Adeyemo, Frankline Agbor, and Gisele Ndoungo.

I would like to thank those who were also inspirational as I stepped into the world of Harriet E. Wilson: Amanda Blunt, Evan Blunt, Sarah Ruffing Robbins, Barbara McCaskill, Carla L. Peterson, Ralph Bauer, Joycelyn Moody, Anne Frey, Kurk Gayle, Cassie Smith, Wendy Roberts, April Langley, Jenny Factor, Marta Werbanowska, Latorial Faison, Tyechia Thompson, Hassan Dasdemir, Donna Daniel, Gilmore and Joy Hurst, Anton Thomas, Eunice Carter, Evette Layne-Linton, Rebecca John, Toya Richardson, Twilla Coates, Joy Thomas, Constance Thomas, Barb Murray, and Dorothy Drummond.

I would also like to remember all the Carters, including the family in Jamaica, with shining spirits like Inez Callum. All the Clarkes in Alberta are a supportive force, including Alston and Anita Clarke, Nell Marshall, Amorette Bradshaw, Sara Gabriel, Chris Clarke, and James Clarke.

I would also like to thank all the Clarkes in the United Kingdom, including Reg, Val, Hiram, Jackie, and Natalie. Parnell Rhule, Ann Bain, Maz Rhone, Hyacinth and Katrina Campbell, Adrian Mayers, Steve Wood, Doreen Boddey, Ian, and Janet Ellis have also supported me on my artistic path. They are also part of the family from the United Kingdom. I would also like to thank all of the Duggans, who are a shining light.

There are many people who are also a part of my artistic journey — to everyone, I thank you for your encouragement and support.

About the Author

Alison Clarke is an award-winning author and a poet. She holds a Master's degree in Children's Literature from Hollins University. In her home of Alberta, Canada, and abroad, Alison immerses herself in nature, writing, and travelling.

Alison is the author of the young adult fantasy series, The Sisterhood. She won the 2016 Writer Of The Year award from Diversity magazine for The Sisterhood, Book One, a novel about Oppie, a sorceress' daughter, her best friend, a dragon, and the journey they go on to save the universe. The Sisterhood Series features themes of the power of the Collective force, the power of art, and features girls and women, especially those of colour, as protagonists. Alison is also an award-winning visual artist, receiving awards for the paintings of her characters featured at the Art Gallery Of Alberta, University Of Alberta, at an art show in Roanoke, Virginia, and other art shows in Canada and internationally.

For her work, both literary and visual art, Alison received the Fil Fraser Award in 2020 from the National Black Coalition Of Canada Society. Most recently, in 2023,

Alison received the Creative And Performing Artists And Writers Fellowship from the American Antiquarian Society. She was awarded the fellowship for her research about Harriet E. Wilson, the subject of her historical fiction series, and the first person of colour to publish a novel.

Alison believes that all forms of art – literary, visual, and so on – can change the world. Being a Writer-In-Residence at the Lotus Art Gallery, from September to December 2016 and teaching creative writing classes was an inspiring experience for Alison, and she has taught creative writing and visual art through other various organizations. Being awarded another Writer-In-Residence position from the Alexandra Writers' Centre in 2021 was another accomplishment for Alison, as she enjoys mentoring up-and-coming writers. Alison also enjoys performing spoken word and has been a performer at Black Arts Matter, a festival in Edmonton featuring black spoken word artists, as well as other local events.

Travelling to other festivals around the world has also captivated Alison, as she believes that travelling is magical and mystical. She has been to conventions in London, England, meeting authors from around the world who write in various genres such as fantasy or science fiction. Alison has done readings and book signings, as well as writing workshops at various conventions and festivals such as Edge Lit 8 in Derby, England. She enjoys meeting people and talking about the magic of Story.